Devil's Orchestra

Sydney Molare

ISBN 0-9765619-1-3
Library of Congress Control Number: 2006923410

This book is printed on acid free paper.

Printed in the United States of America

Publisher: **Fishbowl International, Inc.**
"Viewing Life From All Angles"
PO Box 362
Roxie, MS
www.fishbowlinternational.com

"Viewing Life From All Angles"

Roxie, Mississippi

Other books by Sydney Molare

Somewhere In America

Changing Faces, Changing Places

Small Packages

Grandmama's Mojo *Still* Working

www.sydneymolare.com

This book is dedicated to my parents,
Dr. and Mrs. Charles and Carol Tillman,
who always believed in teaching us the proper and correct way
things should be done. If we deviated, it was on us.
Love you forever…

Devil's Orchestra

www.sydneymolare.com

Tab McGrifth

1

WJZU screeched with activity—phones rang, voices boomed out messages, people zigged and zagged. As the number one station on the Eastern seaboard, it was all in a day's work.

The double doors banged open. An imposing, white-haired figure stood just inside, arms akimbo, his aura nearly visible to the naked eye. It wasn't that he was extremely handsome, because he wasn't. The timeworn face was often described as plainer than plain and the paunchy body, definitely not pin-up material. However, it was the POWER emanating from Tab McGrifth which made people take notice…just as they did now.

His mouth lifted at the corner; hard eyes surveyed the room, his lair, his domain. Conversations interrupted or halted as people greeted him—lips pulled back in pleasure or in some cases, fear. For Tab was what one would call "The Franchise." The top radio personality on the East Coast, his program *Living Life as Your Right* was carried in more than two thousand stations worldwide. Advertisers, the lifeblood of any station, loved him. In fact, two nearly came to blows trying to waggle one of his commercial spots.

He was a cash cow and he knew it. Hell, the world knew it. Station owners from New York City, LA and London practically drooled oceans trying to court him away. Not for Tab, though. He was a big fish in a pretty big pond and he liked it that way. No way would he risk everything he had, what he had worked and cheated to get, for *maybe* more. To say he was totally indispensable without a major "F" up—and even that was debatable—was an understatement.

With a strut of learned arrogance, he moved further into the room. Hearty slaps peppered his back; lips stretched even further, distaste swallowed behind porcelain veneers. Tab barely acknowledged the giver; accepted the fawning as his due.

A studio technician scuttled towards Tab, stopping six feet shy. "Ah, ah…we're ready if you are," he mumbled, eyes shifting behind, above and beside Tab. He didn't have the guts to look him straight on…few people did.

"Lead on, son! My people want to hear from me!" Tab boomed.

"Ah, ah, yessir." The stuttering tech stumbled over his feet and crashed into a waiting desk. Face beet red, he snapped back upright, ignored the coffee he'd spilt on the secretary sitting at the desk—as well as her papers—and threw open the studio door. Tab winked at the pissed woman but offered no assistance. *That* was beneath him.

As he entered the door to the studio, a voice stopped him. "Mr. McGrifth. Wait!"

What the hell? Tab glanced at the clock above the door. Only five minutes before air time. Anybody that had been at the station more than a day *knew* he arrived ten minutes before his program aired, accepted five minutes of compliments and brown nosing then entered the studio promptly at five until. He prided himself on a live broadcast. Being a minute late or taping his program early was *not* an option. His egomaniac opinion: Canned stuff was for woozies. And he'd be *damned* if they called him one.

Lips sneered, eyes narrowed, he turned to confront the voice. "Yes? Make it quick!"

The tech edged further into the studio, crossed his legs and discreetly pushed on his now irritable bladder.

The room mimicked a tomb—eyes riveted, mouths hushed—as a too perky, too young woman ran up and handed him a note. "This person said it was *very* important they speak to you immediately," she gushed, head bobbing like a duck.

Stopped for a message? Tab's eyebrows lifted heavenward. *God, she must be an intern.* "Is that it?" he asked, since the woman still bobbled before him.

"Yes. *Very* important," she nodded her assent before continuing, "I got the feeling you should really call him before you go on air and since you just got here and all, maybe you could take a minute and see what he wants. Follow up and all. I'd hate for it to be an emergency and you didn't talk to them—"

"Thank you," Tab interrupted, ready to get the hell away from the babbling woman. "Thank you very much ah…ah…"

"Sally," she finished for him.

"Thank you, Sally. I'll give them a call as soon as I can." Tab turned to leave.

"Good. Oh, I forgot to tell you," Tab glanced back, a tart remark tickling the edge of his tongue. "I just *love* your show. It's the best." Sally winked with this statement.

"Yes, it is, isn't it? Thank you, again, ah…"

"Sally," she supplied again.

"Sir, you only have three minutes until airtime," the tech squeaked out. He wouldn't have interrupted at all except he knew if Tab were late he'd lead the unemployment line by morning.

"Yes, thank you, Sally."

Tab entered the studio, the unread note jammed into his pocket.

#

The program went off without a hitch. Tab patronized, gushed and fawned over his guest, The Honorable Judge P. Hiram Hirsch. Didn't matter that Judge Hirsch was often his guest, it was a matter of principle since he stood for everything Tab held important—the Christian right wing and tough justice for juvenile lawbreakers amongst the foremost.

After the Judge exited, Tab took a moment to visit his office. His importance to the station was mirrored in his suite—top grade leather furniture, a granite desk, adjoining bedroom with bath and most importantly, a bank of windows which allowed him to survey the city and the mountains behind.

He grabbed an imported cigar before he sifted through his messages. That smoking was prohibited in a public building was of no importance to him. Hell, he was the reason they were able to keep the light on for Christ's sake.

As he threw messages deemed unimportant into the trash can, he heard the crackle of paper in his pocket. *Ah, the message that silly girl gave me*, he thought as he fished it out. Hmmm. It was from Whitehall Fordham. Whitey Ford as Tab called him.

An old mentor from his first station WDMN, Whitey took a young, inexperienced DJ—as Tab was at the time—and molded him into the man he was today. Every thing Tab still did had Whitey's touch on it—his views, mannerisms and most importantly, his power moves.

With eager fingers, Tab dialed the number. Whitey answered with his customary greeting.

"Talk." One word, always.

"Whitey. Tab McGrifth here."

" 'Bout damn time you called back. I expected to hear from you more than an hour ago," Whitey growled.

"Just got the message," Tab lied.

"You should fire that girl I gave it to then. It was something important and she's just walking around with it. In fact, I stressed how important it was so she should have told you."

That Sally had told him exactly that didn't pass Tab's lips. "Rest assured, I'll deal with it in a few minutes. So why'd you call?"

Tab heard Whitey's long, deep sigh before he answered. "Well…the fact is I need to talk to you. Need to get some things off of my chest that's been held in too long. *Way* too long. I need to explain…just…we need to talk."

Tab was puzzled. Whitey Ford admitting he needed a confidant was nothing short of a miracle. That he wanted the confidant to be Tab was mind boggling. "Okay," Tab began slowly, "Where do you want to meet?"

"There's a pub just out of town, *The Shoat's Head.* Meet me there around eight."

Tab sifted through his mind bank. "I've never heard of this pub before. Where is it?"

"Old Hwy. 92 South. The new highway by-passed it so it's not so easy to spot anymore."

Tab scribbled the information on a pad. "I'll find it. What time again?"

"Eight o'clock on the dot."

"I'll be there."

"See that you do."

"Whitey?"

"Ah huh?"

"It's good hearing from you. See you tonight?"

"Bye."

Tab leaned back in the chair, euphoria making his blood hum. He absently fondled himself as he was wont to do whenever something made him pulse, feel alive.

What was that girl's name again? Susie...no, Sally. That's it. Sally.

Tab reached for the phone. Perhaps his newest fan would enjoy showing him just how much she *truly* liked his show...on her knees, of course.

Deva

2

The music was loud, the beat thumping.

"Would you cut that off?" The young woman lying across the lounge whined at her companion. "I'm sick of hearing it! Matter of fact, I'm sick of everything. Ugh!" she ranted before she covered her head with a pillow.

Lena, her assistant/personal secretary/Girl Friday, rolled her eyes. *What's she tired of anyway? Being the number one pop star in the world? Selling millions of albums? Anyone would just about kill their mother to be in her shoes and she's tired of it. Well, just let me get the chance and I'll definitely show more appreciation than this.*

Lena sauntered over and turned down the music anyway. "That good?" she smirked.

"Yeah," the muffled voice replied. "Don't they want to play anything else on these stations?"

"Girl, you know they play only the top songs and right now you're hot and have been for the past few years. You'd be fit to be tied if they didn't play your music and we both know it."

A tousled, blond-streaked head emerged followed by gold, feline eyes set in a narrow face. A face splashed worldwide from billboards, television stations and magazines in various looks, styles and poses. Deva, hip hop princess extraordinaire. Her bullet ride to the top of the pop charts had oft been described as phenomenal. Her voice placed in the realms of the angels.

Early on, people assumed that there was nothing behind the looks and great voice. But she'd proved them wrong. Deva's net worth was now in the nine digit range thanks to her shrewd business mind. Her signature clothes could be spotted on the backs and behinds of millions of adoring fans, and her perfume, Devaour, flew off the shelves.

"And you know this. Shit!" Covers were flung back and the voluptuous body—nearly as recognizable without the face—was revealed. "What do I have planned for today anyway?"

Lena retrieved the PDA always by her side and pressed the front with her stylus. "Looks like you have an interview in two hours at a television station, lunch with some studio execs then another interview—this one radio—after that. Nothing's scheduled for tonight though."

"Thank God! I need some rest right about now. This tour has worn me out."

And it had. A nine million dollar set and fifty cities in three months would wear out anyone...if not for the expected sixty million dollar payoff in the end. It wore out the staff too, but unlike Deva, they wouldn't get anywhere near sixty million. Lena held her tongue and waited.

"Can't you cancel everything and I sleep in?" Deva moaned.

Lena shrugged. "Wish I could but you know sucking up is a requirement not an elective."

"Shit!" Deva ran fingers through her mane. "I am drained. *Drained*, I tell you. I'll be *so* glad when this whole tour thing is finished and I can spend some of that money my accountant says we're making."

"It'll be here soon, chick. Just keep singing and packing them in and time will fly by."

"That's easy for you to say. You aren't up there on stage with the hot lights, costume changes and fans that get out of control." Deva shuddered as she relived the crazed fan that ran up on stage and managed to tear her shirt from her back before the guards reached them. "That was the worst."

"I was there, remember?" Lena replaced her stylus before walking towards the door. "I've got to check on some things for tomorrow. You want to shower and I'll send Cayman over in fifteen?" Cayman was Deva's hair stylist. His flaming personality often clashed with Lena's no nonsense one. Nonetheless, they managed to temper their anger in Deva's presence. She hated petty arguments and neither one of them was looking for a one-way ticket to the house.

"How about I take a shower and you tell Cayman I ran away." Deva grinned.

"Naw. He'd just cuss me out and find you anyway," Lena groused.

"You're right, too." Deva's laughter tinkled in the air. "I guess we'll just go with your first plan—me shower, then Cayman."

"Good. I'll be back in thirty minutes or so. Get to moving."

"I'm moving. I'm moving."

The door closed and Deva slumped back into the covers. The pillow followed and covered her face, all thoughts of a shower gone.

#

The ringing cell phone woke her. Deva tried to ignore it but the *Mission Impossible* tune it shrieked wouldn't allow it. *Where is Lena when you need her?* Rolling the covers back, she slid her lace-covered torso from the lounge.

Where is the damn phone? The ringing seemed to be coming from the direction of the chair in the corner. She grabbed her purse first. No phone. Next, the clothes in the chair. No phone. "Where the hell is it!" She finally located it between the boots she had worn the night before. Just as she reached for it, it fell silent.

"Great! Just dammit great!" Deva pushed the Menu button and groaned as she read CALLER ID BLOCKED. *Shoot that could be anybody.* Dropping the phone, she walked back to the lounge, intending to continue her sleep party. Just as she gave the pillows a final fluff before reclining on them, the phone began singing again.

"Argh! Who the hell can this be!" Deva yelled to herself. Tromping to the blinking phone, she stared at the screen. CALLER ID BLOCKED. She stabbed the button.

"Hello?"

"Yes, Lenora?" a male voice asked.

Who in the world is this? Only a few people, usually family and close friends, called her by her given name. The rest used Deva. "Ah, yes?"

"How's it going?"

"Ah…fine…ah…" Deva had no clue to who she was speaking with but after a fan had stalked and killed that actor, she was always cautious when dealing with unknown people on the phone.

"You don't know who this is, do you?"

The voice seemed familiar but…"Not even a clue," she finally admitted.

"I can tell. Let me help you out. It's Ed. Ed Burris. You know, your old running buddy?"

And did she. She and Ed Burris managed to get into more than their share of trouble from grade school until they graduated. Over the years, they had progressed from water balloons and silly pranks to slipping out of windows—a stunt that got her behind reddened and grounded for six months. But Ed had been more than her partner-in-mischief, he was also the tenor to her alto. They'd sung a million and one duets, winning every talent contest they entered.

When Ed wanted the relationship to go beyond platonic, Deva rebuffed him and their buddy days died a slow, painful death. They'd drifted apart and begun avoiding each other. She'd finally lost touch with him once they went off to college.

As the memories washed over her, she exclaimed, "Oh, my goodness…Ed! How are you?"

"Great. Bet you're wondering how I got this number, huh?"

"Uh ugh. I know Mama probably gave it to you." Her mother always said Ed would make Deva a great husband if she would give him a chance.

"Congratulations! You're the grand prize winner!" Ed mimicked a commentator.

"I knew it. Mama is always giving out my cell phone number. I've heard from so many folks that said we went to school together I threatened to change it and not give it to her. Where'd you see her anyway?"

"At her favorite store—Wal-Mart."

"Now you know that's everybody's favorite store. If Wal-Mart doesn't have it, then nobody does."

"You're right, too." They both laugh at this. "Hey, the reason I'm calling is, I'm in town and I really need to see you. It's been only, what, five years or so?"

"Gosh, yeah. Right after graduation." Deva remembered the stilted conversation followed by an awkward hug at the post-graduation party; the hungry eyes which tugged at her heart. But Ed was just too...familiar. She wanted and needed something more. A more that Ed just didn't possess for her.

"So if you've got time, let's meet. There a tavern just out of town called the *Shoat's Head.* I don't think you'd be recognized if we went there. You can't wear your flashy clothes, but if you dress regularly and clean some of that war paint off your face—"

"War paint!" Deva wailed.

"Yes, war paint. I don't know why you slather that mess over your face when all you need is Noxzema and cocoa butter."

Ed had always hated how Deva dolled herself up for the contests. But stage presence was a must and makeup was part of her stage presence. "I'll have you know I pay somebody forty thousand dollar a year for my makeup."

"Your accountant should be shot on sight."

"Quit." Deva giggled a bit before her gaiety sobered. "Ed…is something wrong?"

"Wrong? No. Why?"

"Well…I mean…we haven't kept in touch or anything and…you just call me out of the blue."

"I caught your show and wanted to see how you were doing in person. That's all."

Relief flooded Deva's body. She was afraid he had bad news he needed to tell her face-to-face. "Oh. Well yes, I can meet you. You're lucky that I have a free night."

"You know I always had great timing." He chuckled.

"Yes, you did. So what's the name of the place again?"

"*The Shoat's Head.* It's a tavern on old Hwy. 92. Your driver shouldn't have any trouble finding it but you probably shouldn't arrive in a limo. That would be a dead giveaway for you."

"Right."

"I'll see you, what, around eight or so?"

"That's fine. Ed…great talking to you again."

"I can't wait to see you in person. Until tonight?"

"Tonight."

"Bye."

Deva recradled the phone. *Ed wants to see me again.* Even though she'd never wanted Ed for anything more than a friend, there was an allure to knowing that a man she hadn't seen in years still wanted to see her for some reason. Maybe it was the fame…maybe not. Either way, she planned to give him something to remember her by.

Deva flung open the door. "Lena!" she screamed at the top of her lungs.

Juan Rodriguez

3

The Latin face concentrated on the computer screen while his fingers flew over the keyboard, frantically keeping pace with the scene playing out in his head. The unexpected way the chapter unfolded had him hunched over, pecking furiously, the world blocked out. His knew his editor was going to have an early martini after reading this material!

And he would. Juan Rodriguez was the current "Golden Boy" of Oscan House books. They had taken a chance on an unknown author, with a controversial manuscript, and it had paid off in spades. His novel, *See Me for Me*—written by a gay man about gay culture—had amazingly, shot to the top of bestseller's lists across the country.

Accolades were heaped on him left and right. Gay activists trumpeted the book as the new "Alternative Lifestyle" bible. The books flew off the shelves and the money poured in. His sophomore novel, *Two Daddies,* followed the same course. All and all, Juan's star was shining pretty bright in the literary world right now.

He was so engrossed in the scene, the closing door of the front door barely registered. Not until hands touched him and a small voice said "Daddy, I'm home!" did he reluctantly tear his eyes away while his hands continued on autopilot.

"Hey, Loam!" Juan squealed at the cherubic face staring into his.

Loam pulled himself into his father's lap and gave the biggest hug a five-year-old could. Juan smiled back at the child, love glistening from his eyes, and tousled Loam's hair. "Where's your other papa?"

"I'm right here, Babe," a voice answered.

Juan smiled as the man stepped into sight. Zeus. His partner for life. Six feet and muscular, Zeus was the poster child for tall, dark and handsome. Juan always thought it should be tall, dark and pretty because he *was* man-pretty with his long eyelashes and lush lips. Juan swung Loam onto his hip as he stood and hugged Zeus.

Zeus pulled back and stared at the computer screen. "I see you've been working since we left."

"Yep, almost got two chapters done. Matter of fact, would have had three if you guys hadn't arrived."

"Saved by your boys." Zeus laughed, showing a row of perfect teeth.

"That what boys are for…amongst other things." Juan wiggled his eyebrows.

Loam patted Juan's face focusing his attention back to him. "Can we watch *Power Rangers* now?" His eyes pleaded.

"Sure," Zeus replied before Juan could answer. "Let's just get out of your daddy's hair and you and me can bond some more."

Loam transferred from one set of arms to the other. "What's bond mean, Daddy?"

Zeus' response was lost as they turned the corner. Juan settled back at his keyboard, his mind already returning to his scene. *Let's see, where was I?* As he reread his writing and sifted through his mental notes, the YOU'VE GOT MAIL! icon popped onto the screen. With a perfunctory double click, the message opened.

Message dated 1/12

From: Bodie40@zapnet.net

To: Juan Rodriguez

Hey. Long time, no speak. Sorry how things went down. Please forgive. We need to talk. Face to face. Guess you might not want to talk to me but I need to SEE you. So, dump Romeo and meet me at the Shoats Head Tavern out on old 92 at 8.

Bodie :)

Juan's chest slammed to the floor, breath nearly ceased as he read, then reread the email.

Bodie. English professor, advisor…Juan's first lover. Blond, beach-boy tanned, model's body…he was everything Juan wanted *except* he put the w-h-o-r in whore. He'd taken Juan's love then used, abused and dismissed him without a backwards glance. God, how he'd loved him.

He couldn't stop his eyes from reading the message for a fourth time. *Why now,* just when life was going so well. Didn't matter that Juan Rodriguez had sold millions of books, had all the money he needed, a man he loved and a son…Bodie still managed to pop up like a stinking, dead fish.

"Babe, wanna order pizza tonight?" Zeus' voice drifted out, his footfall coming closer.

As Juan jumped to click the email closed, he upset the glass of cola next to the keyboard and soda gushed across the keys. "Damn!"

"Hey, what happened?"

Juan grabbed a dishtowel and began mopping at the keyboard. "Nothing. Just spilled my drink."

"Damn. Let me help." Zeus grabbed some paper towels and turned to offer assistance.

"No!" Juan stood stiffly in front of the computer, arms outstretched.

Zeus looked askance at him. "The soda will make the keys stick." Zeus shifted to the left. Juan blocked his progress. "What's wrong with you?"

"Nothing." *Calm down and sound normal.* "It's just that I don't want to mess up what I've written so far and you know swiping at the keys will do that and then I'd have to start all over." The explanation sounded lame even to his ears.

"Yeah, right." Zeus shifted right. Juan blocked left.

"I've got it. Really. I can…I can take care of this." *God, please don't let me accidentally pop that email open! Not now.*

Zeus stared into Juan's eyes, the "something's wrong" look on his face and sighed. "What's the deal, Juan?"

"Nothing. Why?" Juan rocked from foot to foot.

"You sure? I mean, I just wanted to help and you're acting strange."

Juan slid a shaky smile on. "You know how wigged out I get when I'm working. It's just that this project is so important and…" Juan stepped to take Zeus into his arms, "…and I don't want anything to go wrong. You know we *are* spending the advance on this baby already," he laughed.

Zeus hugged him back. "That is true."

"So just let me take care of this little accident and you go on back with Loam. OK?"

"All right." Zeus pulled from the embrace, no trace of worry evident on his face. "So, do you want pizza for dinner or what?"

"Oh." Juan turned his back and began mopping at the desktop. "I think I'm going out to the poetry reading at *Zinzibaz*." The deep need, no want, to see Bodie one last time forced him to lie.

Zeus cocked an eyebrow. "Really? I thought you were going to pass on that."

"I was but it's important to keep the exposure up, you know." Sweat popped on his forehead. He felt a bead coursing through his hair on the way to rolling down his face as Zeus stared at him. After a few tense seconds, Zeus replaced the smile and said, "Yeah, I do know. Well, what time do you think you'll be home?"

Juan shrugged. "I imagine around ten or so."

"OK. I guess me and Loam will just have to split the pizza."

"Save a slice for me, will you?"

"You know I will. Let me let you get back to work." Zeus gave him a peck on the lips then left.

Juan sent a hasty reply before he shut off the computer and carefully mopped at the keys. As he did, he couldn't shake the feeling that he had just made the biggest mistake of his life.

Tab McGrifth

4

The fog was heavy on old Hwy. 92. No lights were visible, no cars had passed. Tab drove slowly, body tensed, eyes straining for stray animals along the sides of the road. The last thing he needed was for a damn deer to hit his Mercedes convertible.

He sighed in relief as he spotted a glow of neon up ahead. The *Shoat's Head Tavern* sign came into view.

The establishment itself was a disappointment—a seen-better-days building no bigger than a tract house with a gravel parking lot. Three cars were parked there already.

Why the hell did Whitey want me to meet him all the way out here?

The gravel crunched loudly as Tab slowly navigated the lot watching for beer bottles. Parking near the door, he heaved his bulk out and looked around. The air was acrid from the smoke billowing out of the chimney atop of the building. A skinny dog sniffed around trash cans propped and overflowing beside the building. With a sigh, Tab headed toward the front door.

The inside was just as pitiful as the outside. A large bar was positioned by the door and mixed-matched tables and chairs seemed to be randomly placed around the remainder of the small room whose focal point was a huge fireplace. From what Tab could see, only three people were inside—two men at the bar and the bartender who sported a Mohawk, muscle shirt and earrings embedded along his lobe.

What the hell kind of place is this?

If Tab were honest with himself, he would realize that his reaction was born from a fear that had plagued him since he'd left his poverty-stricken beginnings: That one day he'd slide back down the ladder to end where he'd begun.

"Evening. Welcome to the *Shoat's Head Tavern*," the bartender greeted him lazily.

"Evening." Tab inclined his head.

"What'll you have?"

"Nothing right now. I'm waiting for someone."

The bartender indicated a seat. Tab slid onto the stool and nodded at the men sitting there. Both of them looked like they were on hard times—bad haircuts, polyester suits, shirts with ties pulled away, and scuffed shoes. Tab dismissed them without another glance. He'd lived in the lap of luxury too long to remember when he had been their identical twin.

"Nasty night out there, isn't it?" one of the men said. Tab turned towards the voice. He stared at the speaker's dirty blond hair before traveling down to the craggy, pitted face.

"Yeah," he said before glancing away.

"If you don't mind me asking, who are—"

"I mind," Tab growled and shifted on the stool, his back now to the man.

The man held his hands in front of him. "Sorry, bub. No harm meant."

"No offense taken."

All eyes turn as the door opened…

Deva

5

No one would recognize the woman riding in the back seat of the Pontiac Grand Am. Minimal makeup, plain clothes and a short black wig ensured that.

"Jarrel, are we almost there?" Deva hugged herself as she stared out in the darkness. They hadn't seen a house or lights for miles.

"I'm not sure, Ms. Deva, but the guy at the tavern said to stay on old 92 for ten miles and we should see the sign." Jarrel stared at her in the rear-view mirror. Though he'd never admit it, he was apprehensive about this whole setup. Seems like if some old friend wanted to see Ms. Deva, he could have come to the hotel. No need to drag her way out to the boondocks. He shifted his eyes back to the road.

"How many miles have we gone? It must have been at least ten by now."

Jarrel glanced at the dashboard. "Only eight. I've got the counter set so I could keep track."

"If we don't see something soon, we're turning around."

We should have just stayed at the hotel. But Jarrel didn't voice his opinion. He was paid to drive and protect, not give advice.

A neon light seemed to spring out of nowhere, surprising him. Jarrel braked hard, throwing Deva against the side. "What's wrong!" she screamed as the car skidded to a stop.

"Sorry about that. The place just seemed to sneak up on me. Guess I didn't spot it in the fog and all."

"Oh, we're here?" Deva straightened and glanced out of the window. The *Shoat's Head Tavern* sign glowed back at her. Her nose wrinkled at the scene before her—a raggedy old hole-in-the-wall building just like the juke joints she'd left behind in Mississippi. *How the hell did Ed find this place?*

Jarrel studied the area. "This is it. Not too much to it, is there?"

"Doesn't look like it. Well, just park and I'll see what Ed wants and we'll be out of here in a minute."

"Let me get close to the front door. Don't look like they get much traffic, so I'm gonna just park right out front."

"That's fine."

Jarrel parked and slid out to open Deva's door. She looked at him in surprise as he offered his arm. "What?"

"I'm not letting you go in there alone. I'm here to protect, too."

"You don't have to do that. I'll be fine." She waved him off and began walking towards the front door.

Jarrel's hand stopped her. "I'm sorry, Ms. Deva, but either I go with you or I'm taking you back to the hotel. You can fire me in the morning."

Deva stared at his stoic, unmoving face. In all the years he'd been driving her, she'd never seen him this way before. After a few seconds, she took the proffered arm. "We'll do it your way, but I don't think it's necessary."

"I know you don't, but this way, I would sure feel better about things."

"I understand. Let's get on inside."

Jarrel pushed the door open…

Juan Rodriguez

6

Juan's heart thumped in his chest. He was a fool and he knew it. He'd lied to Zeus to drive out to God knows where to see an old don't-give-a-shit-about-him lover.

Bodie writes a damn email and I jump like I'm still his love flunky.

His attention was split between the road and the rear view mirror. The fact that he'd seen nothing resembling human or animal existence since exiting onto this stretch of highway made him edgy. Maybe it was the weather. The heavy fog and now drizzle would keep the animals in the woods where they could stay dry. He knew he should turn the car around and write Bodie out of his life for good...but he couldn't. On some subconscious level, he *needed* this closure, needed to get him out of his system for all eternity.

"God, just let me be strong when I see him. I don't want to make an ass of myself like I did before," Juan prayed aloud as he remembered the last meeting with Bodie. A begged for reunion evolved into a flash lovefest quickly turned loathfest when Bodie jetted out while Juan slept. "I just want to see what he wants and that's the end of it. Please let me get out of here safe and please, *please* don't let Zeus find out. Amen."

His mind was so jumbled he barely registered he'd reached the tavern. The neon sign seemed to sprout out of nowhere as he passed it. He cursed his lack of concentration as he slowed and backed up.

There were four cars in the parking lot and one out front of the run-down building.

This looks like something you see on a documentary.

Nevertheless, he pulled behind the Grand Am parked in front and cut the engine. With a deep breath, he opened the door then closed it quickly. He rummaged around in the glove compartment a minute before he found what he was searching for. Placing the beads in his pocket, he reopened the door and strolled to the entrance. After another glance around, he pushed the door open...

Tab McGrifth

7

Interested eyes drank in the sight of the young, black couple coming through the door. Tab gave them a once-over and dismissed them. She was probably a prostitute and he, some married sucker trying to get as far away from anybody that might see them. Without a word to anyone, they settled at one of the tables near the fire.

Tab glanced at the Budweiser clock over the bar. Seven fifty. Whitey should be here any minute.

"Hey Bartender, give me a Coors if you've got one."

"Sure. Want a glass with that?" The Bartender asked as he wiped the counter with a dirty rag.

Tab looked at the dust-laced glasses hanging over the bar then the Mohawked man. "Got a plastic cup?"

The bartender smirked before reaching under the bar and placing a cellophane-wrapped Holiday Inn cup on the counter. The Coors followed.

"That'll be seven-fifty."

The hand reaching for his wallet stilled. *How the hell was a dollar-fifty beer worth seven-fifty in this hellhole?* "Little stiff, don't you think?" Tab barked.

"The plastic cup makes things cost a little more," the bartender deadpanned.

"It's not even your bar's cup, for Christ's sake."

"Because we *imported* it in, it costs more. You want the beer or not?" The bartender reached for the Coors.

Tab pulled it away. "I want it." He threw a ten on the counter.

"Keep the change?" the bartender pushed.

"Nope and here's your tip: Quit ripping people off." Tab poured the contents of the bottle into the cup and ignored the glare from the man. Seemed like this bar might need some free "advertisement" on his show. This thought made him smile.

The door pushed open and Tab turned yet again…

Deva

8

Deva and Jarrel faced the door. Jarrel had already done a scope of the tavern and concluded that there was only one way in and one way out—a bad thing if trouble started. Not that he couldn't hold his own. Being six-four and two hundred and fifty pounds made a man think twice before taking him on.

"What a dump! What in the world was Ed thinking when he chose this place? I can't see him even visiting here at all!" Deva whined.

"Yeah, but this is the place." Jarrel kept his eyes trained on the door and the men at the bar. The fat one and the two down-on-their-luck cases didn't seem to be a problem. However, the bartender, who leered and blew kisses at Deva, might be a different case. If he kept on, he might get another hole placed in his body…by force.

"What time is it?" Deva asked while looking at the clock above the bar. "Ed should be here any minute. I sure hope he's not late because I'm not waiting around too long," she huffed.

Jarrel eyed her for a moment before asking quietly, "Who is this guy you agreed to meet here anyway, Ms. Deva?" Normally, he didn't pry into Deva's life, but the way she had dropped everything to meet somebody out in the boonies made him curious.

Deva leaned back in her chair, trying to think of a way to describe why she'd agreed to meet an old friend without giving out too much information. She might be a public personality, but her life was very private and she planned to keep it like that. "Well, Ed is…from my hometown, Yokel, Mississippi."

"So this is somebody from way back."

"Yeah, like from childhood way back."

"Ahuh. Old flame?" Jarrel smiled while he ventured this question.

"No! I mean…I mean Ed *might* have been interested at one time but…nothing ever came of it." Deva wrung her hands, a sure sign she was flustered.

"Ahuh. And?" Jarrel let the remainder of the question hang in the air.

"And what? Ed was in town and just wanted to see me again."

"The hotel wasn't good enough for him?" Jarrel's eyebrows quirked. "Is he running from the law or something?"

The question made Deva pause. She hadn't seen Ed in more than five years and she had no idea of what he might or might not be running from. *God, please don't let me have stepped into some mess.*

"Is that a 'yes, he is' or a 'no, he isn't' or just an 'I don't know?' " Jarrel leaned forward, fingers tented over his nose.

"I don't *know*." Deva forced herself to look into his eyes. "The Ed I remember wouldn't be running from the law. He wasn't…that type of man. Besides, my mother wouldn't have given him my number if he was into some shady stuff."

Jarrell lolled his head as he spoke. "Mamas forget and forgive a lot of things *especially* if they like you."

And that was true. Deva's mother loved herself some Ed. Enough to overlook any wrongdoing on his part? She couldn't be sure. Deva wrapped now shaking arms around her torso. "You might be right, Jarrel, but let's just wait and see for ourselves."

"As you wish." Jarrel leaned back slowly, a look of censure on his face.

Both of them turned as the door opened…

Juan Rodriguez

9

Juan entered what he would have described in one of his novels as a dive—cheap furniture, tacky floors and cheesy patrons. A Mohawked man sporting way too many earrings stood behind a classic bar. The bartender, Juan assumed. The man nodded but offered no greeting. After a quick glance around the room, Juan headed for the rear of the place. No need for anyone to see him with Bodie.

A couple seated near the fire made him pause. She looked familiar but…oh well, he couldn't place her right now. The setting wasn't right. One thing for sure, she looked *way* too high-class for this crappy place.

Juan settled into a booth lining the back wall and slightly out of direct view of the door. He had to be cautious because everything was on the line if Zeus found out where he was…and why. *Lord, please don't let there be any fans here tonight!*

Bits of conversation drifted to him as he drank in the scene before him. He played the 'Guess What They Do' game in an attempt to relax.

Hmmm, the dried up blond man at the counter? Juan betted he was a salesman of some sort. As he glanced at the clock, he surmised that the man either had no wife or didn't want to go home to the wife and family.

The guy sitting next to him with the dark hair— probably in the same field. The way they carried on an easy, loud conversation and the fact that they were nearly identically dressed indicated that they might know each other; be friends.

Now the fat guy a few stools down had him stumped. His clothes looked expensive and his haircut, top notch. Even with his back turned, he exuded power…but here he was in the middle of Podunk, nursing a cheap beer when he looked like he should be holding court in an upscale restaurant. An executive cutting an after-hours deal? But why here? After a few minutes Juan gave up on him.

The couple seemed to be…waiting. The no contact between them indicated either they weren't a pair or that they were having some problems in the relationship. As big as the man was, Juan would definitely say he was professional football player material but his face didn't ring any bells. The woman was gorgeous even with that ugly wig on. Though she kept the shawl wrapped tightly around her, it only emphasized her curves versus camouflaging them. Juan finally decided that she was a model probably in a mess of some sort and the man was helping her out.

The bartender, well, we know what he does. However, the way he kept eyeing the woman *and* the way the man with the woman eyed the bartender made Juan's stomach flip-flop.

Bad Karma there.

Juan wished for the hundredth time he'd never come…or that Bodie would hurry up.

Sydney Molare'

Chapter 10

The lone figure dressed in white seemed to glide to the door. In fact, if the dog beside the building could talk, he'd swear that's exactly what he did—glide. His hackles rose, teeth bared, but a look into the man's eyes sent him scurrying into the woods, tail tucked between his legs.

The man looked around the parking lot and smiled.

All were present and accounted for. Now it was time to pay the piper…

Tab McGrifth

11

Tab sneered as the Hispanic man walked in the door and took a seat in the back.

A greased-back cornholer if I ever saw one. At least he didn't sit next to him. That would have been a problem. A BIG problem.

He nursed his beer a while before glancing at the clock again. One until. Tab turned back to his suds, wondering if old Whitey was still going to show.

Thunder clapped, the building shook mightily and the lights blinked.

"Don't worry, folks. I've got a generator if the power fails," the bartender announced.

The door rattled—gaining everyone's attention—before the knob turned slowly. Expectant eyes were glued to the turning cylinder, hoping the new arrival was for them. Tab held his breath. He *felt* Whitey was about to make his entrance.

A slight, bowed figure walked in. The hair was sparse, age spots visible through the few strands still left. The face was now gaunt—ravaged by whiskey, hard living and too many cigarettes. Though the body was about fifty pounds lighter than Tab remembered, there was still authority in his bearing. Whitey.

Tab jumped from the stool and went to greet him.

"Whitey. Glad to see you." Tab hugged him briefly, wincing when he felt the bony protrusion of his spine through the coat.

"Same here." Rheumy eyes surveyed the room. "Let's grab one of those tables back there so we can talk."

"Want a drink before we get settled?"

"Hell, does a whore want a john? Get me a Jack straight." A rattled cough followed this announcement.

For as long as Tab had known him, that's all Whitey had ever drunk—Jack Daniels, no ice, no water. He turned to the bartender. "One Jack straight."

"Want that in a glass or an *imported* cup?" the bartender fenced.

"A cup. Hell, we don't want him to drink nothing but what he ordered. In fact, give me a fresh pint if you've got one." You could never be too careful in these places.

The bartender slid the cup and pint towards him. Tab quirked an eyebrow, waited for the outlandish bill that was sure to follow this request.

"Twenty seven dollars." The bartender smirked.

Gawddammit! This was highway robbery! But Tab held his tongue and forked out a twenty and a ten. Oh, how he planned to "advertise" this establishment!

He grabbed his purchases and beer then followed a slow-moving Whitey to a table in the back of the room near the "pretty boy". Tab wished Whitey had chosen another table but his other choice would have put him next to the Black couple and that was just as bad. Setting the cup and pint on the table, he helped his old mentor ease into a chair.

"Open it up, boy! I'm chilled to the bones." Another rattled cough.

With quick fingers, Tab poured half a cup of Jack Daniels. Whitey looked puzzled when he offered it to him.

"You can't get no more in there?" he wheezed.

Tab filled the cup to the brim.

"That's more like it." Whitey smiled as his trembling hand pulled the cup to his thin lips. After a long swallow, he smacked wet lips and held out the vessel for more. Tab topped it off.

Whitey gulped this cup almost empty and smacked his lips again. "Ahhh. Now, let's talk."

"Sure." Tab shifted his chair back from the table. "What's so important?"

Whitey's eyes seem to pierce Tab's soul as he stared at him. Then he smiled, showing too white dentures that looked artificial in the bone-skinny face. "Boy, you looking prosperous."

"That a nice way of saying I've put on weight?" Tab guffawed.

"Naw. You look like a man that's made it. You sitting that suit well."

After paying a thousand for the tailor made suit, he should. "Well, thank you, Whitey. Now, what's going on?" Tab hitched an eye at him. *A ruined husk. A carcass. The walking dead.* All these thoughts flitted through his mind as he looked at Whitey. He was careful to keep his thoughts concealed, though.

The old man didn't return the look. Instead he gazed off in the direction of the bar. "You know, I was sitting here remembering the first time I laid eyes on you. You remember?"

Though fifty years had passed, Tab's mind dredged up the memory like it had happened only yesterday. The years in Okracrocabee County put a smile of remembrance on his lips. His parents, old when they had him, raised him in a lean-to shack they white-washed every year to show how much better off they were than the Nigras, as they called them back then. There was the requisite outhouse and the five-acre "garden" that provided the vegetables and fake meat when real meat couldn't be had. He'd spent plenty of time in that garden, the sun baking his neck to the red color of farmers world round.

He'd had no encouragement from his father, and minimal gestures of faith from his mother, but he managed to finish high school. His father's lack of encouragement became anger when Tab told him he wanted to go to college. 'What the hell you gonna learn up there? I need you here,' were his words. To keep the peace, Tab hitched any available ride he could find—old trucks, wagons and once, even a tractor—to Monrie Jr. College every other day and returned early afternoon to help in the fields.

By the time they slapped the diploma in Tab's hands, he had already made up his mind not to live his life based around the Almanac—rain, sunshine or locusts—or the cycles of the moon. He wanted to sleep in a real bed, on real sheets, own more than two pair of pants at a time and piss without fear of an unseen snake biting into his pecker. That piece of paper he'd slaved for was his ticket out.

"Yep. I was a pup fresh out of Junior College and searching high and low for a job. WDMN must have been the sixth station I'd applied to."

"Yeah, you mentioned that. I recall that you had on an ugly seersucker suit that looked like it belonged to your daddy—"

"It did." Tab interrupted, thinking of the harsh words his father had said to his mother when she'd pleaded Tab's case.

"—scruffy shoes and a God-awful cowlick. You couldn't have been more than a hundred and forty pounds wet. I said to myself, 'This boy here is a pure mess!'" Whitey grimaced. "Hell! I could smell the sour milk-ring around you neck. But when I looked into your eyes, I saw the fire. The drive. I *knew* you'd be the one out of a million to make it."

"Seems like you were right, too." Tab poured another finger of whiskey into Whitey's cup before he continued. "I was scared out of my mind that day. Pa had all but told me to get the hell on and I only had twenty dollars to my name. Wouldn't have had that if Mama hadn't snuck it to me while Pa was taking a crap in the outhouse. That satchel I was carrying?" Whitey nodded. "Y'all probably thought I had my resume and important papers in there. Hmmmp. All it had inside was two pairs of patched drawers, my toothbrush and three hog head souse sandwiches wrapped in a greasy paper sack."

"I'll be damn!" Whitey whooped. "And I thought you was trying to impress me."

"I was. Every place I'd been had turned me down. To be honest, WDMN was the last one on my list. I'd told myself if y'all didn't take a chance on me, I was gonna cut out for California or somewhere and see if I could find something out there."

"Everybody's glad you didn't. Shit! You put us on the map!" Whitey nodded. "We would have missed out on one of the, if not *the*, most influential voice on radio."

"I'm glad it didn't turn out that way, too."

"Yep, I got the pick of the litter with you." Whitey knocked on wood. Then, his tone turned serious. "Boy, do you remember what you said? You know, when I was sitting there scratching my chin, thinking about whether or not to offer you the job?"

Tab leaned back in his chair before he hitched his lip and showed his pearly whites. His mind relived that moment with relish. "Sure do." He folded his hands above his heart and recited the words. "I said, 'I'd sell my *soul* to the devil for a chance to work here.'"

"You got that right!" Whitey laughed heartily.

Deva

12

The sexy Puerto Rican seemed to pause as he passed the table. Deva pulled her shawl tighter and turned her head. The last thing she wanted was to be called out by a fan. Not that she had anything against her fans. She just wasn't in the mood to entertain any at this moment.

"Know that guy?" Jarrel asked after he'd followed the man's progress to a table further back.

"I don't think so. I probably look like somebody he knows." Deva shrugged.

"That's easy to believe since everybody thinks they know you now."

The more her visage was splashed across televisions, newspapers and magazines, the more people felt like they were actually friends. "True. The world feels like they are on speaking terms with me," Deva laughed. "Let's just hope he doesn't recognize me. I don't feel up to men drooling over me tonight."

Jarrel leaned close, amusement in his eyes. "I don't think you've got a thing to worry about with that one. You're not his type." He nodded towards the man and blinked his eyelashes rapidly.

Deva's eyes followed. Though not readily evident, she saw the subtle signs she'd missed earlier. "And you're right, too."

Thunder clapped, the building shook mightily and the lights blinked.

"Don't worry, folks. I've got a generator if the power fails," the bartender announced.

The door rattled—gaining everyone's attention—before the knob turned slowly. Expectant eyes were glued to the turning cylinder, hoping the new arrival was for them. Deva held her breath in anticipation.

The man that entered was short, mocha brown and built. Water flowed from his overcoat creating a hazard just inside the door. He pulled a snazzy tam from his head before his eyes zeroed in on Deva.

"Ed! Ed, over here!" Deva rose and clapped her hands in joy. Jarrel rose beside her, his face devoid of expression.

A smile split Ed's face as he walked forward, arms held wide. Deva hesitated for only a second before she launched herself into them. At the first touch, memories washed over her; infused her brain. They stood there tightly embraced, no words, just past history melding them together.

Ed pulled back first. "Hey, girl, you're looking great!" His eyes roved over her.

"I do not! I look like doodoo in this tacky wig and clothes," Deva looked down at her attire then back at him.

Ed had seen her look way worse but tactfully avoided mentioning this fact. "It definitely takes some getting use to." He smiled again.

Movement made him notice the man who stood at the table. He held out his hand. "I'm Ed Burris. Lenora and I go way back."

Jarrel squinted, puzzled. "Who?" He looked at Deva for an answer.

"Lenora is my real name. My family and friends from home still use it," she explained.

"Oh. For a minute there, I thought maybe he had you mixed up with someone else."

"Believe me, there is no way I could mix up Lenora with anyone," Ed assured him and hugged her to his side.

"Hush." She swatted at his shoulder. "Sit down and tell me what's been going on with you."

As Ed seated Deva, Jarrel moved his chair away from the table and closer to the fire. He wanted to give them some semblance of privacy but remain close enough if he was needed.

"So where have you been? What's been going on?" Deva gushed.

"Here and there. I finished up at State and now I'm working on my MBA."

"How are your folks? I rarely get a chance to get home to see anybody anymore." A wistful tone crept into her voice.

Ed shook his head. "Still acting like teenagers. If you see one, you see the other."

"Nothing wrong with that. How about your sisters?"

"Babygirl is almost finished with college."

"Is she really?" Deva mentally calculated the time. "Yeah, she sure is. We're getting old!"

"Only you would think that twenty-three was old."

They giggled conspiratorially before the wistful look returned to Deva's face. "I need to get home and see them. Sounds like things are going well."

"They are," Ed affirmed. "So tell me, how did all this happen?"

"What?"

"The success. The last time I heard, you were still singing at talent contests. Next thing I knew, you'd blown up; stomping with the big dogs." Ed pounded the floor for emphasis. "I mean, you didn't win *Star Search* or *American Idol* but you're big as all get out anyway."

Deva relaxed into her seat. "Well, it all happened so fast. I was approached by this agent after I'd won the talent contest at A & M. I really didn't pay him any attention because I'd been approached before but none of the others had been talking anything worth more than air. They all wanted me to produce a demo *then* they'd see what they could do as far as getting me a record deal." Deva rolled her eyes. "They were nothing but talk basically, because after I'd spent my money for the demo, I heard diddly squat from them."

"Why was this guy different?" Ed queried.

"Hans—his name is Hans Kelfiger—anyway, Hans *worked* on me." Her finger pointed to her chest. "Made promises I was sure he couldn't back up...but he did every last one of them. He was the one that told me to start my own production company and use the record labels as distributors. That way, I'd keep the bulk of my money and he was right."

"That was sound advice. So...what did old Hans get out of the deal?"

"He became my partner."

Ed gave her a dubious look before he shook his head and stared at the ceiling.

His reaction was one she'd seen dozens of times before—mainly when people underestimated her business aptitude—and it irked Deva. "Hey, I didn't have two dimes to rub together. Hans put up the money to set up the production company and bankrolled me until I had my first album ready for distribution."

"And now he gets half of everything you make."

"No. He gets half of all *record* sales I make. The endorsements, clothing line and perfume sales are all mine." Deva gave him a self-satisfied smile.

Ed shrugged then frowned. "Don't you think it's kind of…*strange* how things went down?"

"What do you mean?"

"This *Hans* fellow showing up with his 'Knight in Shining Armor' show to rescue you," he spat out. "Just out of nowhere to offer you the world on a platter."

Ed's skeptical words struck a nerve. Deva bristled. "Ed, if you'd been there, you would have done the same thing I did. Hans didn't just talk the talk. He walked the walk. He laid out a solid plan and put the money on the table. Not later, right then…and…there." Her index finger punctuated her words.

"Ahem." Ed folded his arms across his chest. "He was just helping out just to help out, I guess? No thought about himself? Right."

Deva threw her hands in the air. "Say what you want, but let me tell you this. After Hans showed me the plan then slapped that briefcase of money on the table…I didn't care if he was Old Satan himself 'cause I was going to give *everything* I had to see if he could turn my dreams into reality."

Tension was thick in the air. Finally, a sly smile slid onto Ed's face as he studied her. "Looks like it paid off."

"It has." Deva smiled back, smugly. "Oh, it has."

Juan Rodriguez

13

Juan grew restless and decided to grab a soda. He'd just pulled his legs from beneath the table when thunder clapped, the building shook mightily and the lights blinked.

"Don't worry, folks. I've got a generator if the power fails," the bartender announced.

The door rattled—gaining everyone's attention—before the knob turned slowly. Expectant eyes were glued to the turning cylinder, hoping the new arrival was for them. Juan's heartbeat sped up. He *smelled* Bodie.

A lone man walked inside—slow, liquid, every blonde hair in place despite the weather, tan ever-present.

Juan's gut clenched; palms wetted. Though it had been years, he'd know that walk anywhere. Afterall, it was one of the things that had attracted him in the first place.

Bodie looked around at everyone. Juan rose on shaky legs and spoke with an even shakier voice. "Bodie. Back here."

Bodie's smile reached across the room and Juan felt its impact in his chest. He tried to quell his return smile but couldn't. This was Bodie. His first love.

Their eyes remained locked on each other as he walked across the floor. With each step, more good memories spouted to the forefront of Juan's brain. He clutched the rosary in his pocket as Bodie neared the table. *Lord give me strength!*

"Heyyyy. You're looking good!" Bodie's silky voice embraced Juan as he held open arms wide.

Juan hesitated only a moment before he walked into the embrace. "You too." Though he'd never admit it in a million years, Bodie *felt* good, too.

Bodie settled into a chair without waiting for an offer to sit. "How are things going or should I ask?"

"Fine. Everything's just fine."

"So I'm reading." Juan was surprised he'd kept up with his developments. Afterall, their breakup was not in the least amicable. "You've got a little boy now, don't you?"

"Yes, Loam. He's five going on fifty." Juan laughed, thinking about Loam's antics.

"That's how they say it goes. Born today, tomorrow, fifty. I wouldn't know because I'm still fatherless." Bodie winked.

Juan looked away. Bodie's dislike of kids was well known…especially to Juan. He cleared his throat. "Sorry to hear that."

"Hell, you know I never cared about kids. Too much trouble. Besides, I would either have to sleep with a woman—*you* know that's out—or go through an adoption agency. To be honest, I don't think my background check could hold up if they started digging," Bodie stated matter-of-factly.

He was right. Though he was a university professor, he'd had past skirmishes with the police that often had the Dean calling him on the carpet.

"You could have donated sperm and had someone have a child for you."

"A surrogate? Shit, from what I see on TV, half of them let you spend all your money on the bills then they want to keep the kid anyway. A free ride if you ask me."

Juan knew what he meant. He and Zeus had experienced that exact situation with their first try at having a child. Thank goodness they'd hit pay dirt with the second one. "Not all of them are like that. You've just got to be super selective."

"Is that what you did?" Bodie searched his face.

"Yeah. I wasn't interested in sleeping with a woman and I damn sure wasn't up for my partner to be either. Something about my *past.*" Hurtful images made the sarcasm drip from Juan's lips.

Bodie winced. The barb had hit its mark. "Can't forget it, can you?"

The bad memories flooded Juan's brain; made him suddenly irritated. "Sometimes it's difficult," he barked.

Bodie scrutinized Juan's face thoroughly before he finally asked, "Want something to drink? I'm parched." He stood from the chair.

His switching gears like that threw Juan for a second. "I'll have a Coke if they have one. If not, get me a beer."

Bodie walked his signature walk as he went for the drinks. Juan watched the firm hips sway, unaware he was doing so until he felt the front of his pants stretching.

Damn!

Watching Bodie's return walk made it stretch even further.

"You're in luck. The bartender gave me his last Pepsi." Bodie smiled as he set the drink in front of Juan . "I know you love Coke but this will have to do for now."

"That's fine." Juan discreetly rearranged his crotch before he popped the top and took a long swallow.

Bodie poured his beer into a glass. "So, how'd you get so lucky? Normally, it takes an author years to get where you are."

Juan set his can on the table, glad for the turn in conversation. "As the old saying goes: 'Right place. Right time.' "

"That simple, huh?"

"No, it wasn't that simple but after we…split…" Juan looked away from the pale, probing eyes, "I put my feelings on paper then found an agent to shop it around."

"And it was a done deal."

Juan shook his head. "Not really. My agent, Nancy Rottenburg—awesome woman by the way—didn't think that it would be easy to find my manuscript a 'home'. Hell, I didn't either. A book by a professed gay man about other gay men? Definitely not mainstream material."

"Right." Bodie waved him on.

"But somebody thought it was. Both she and I were floored when the offer came in from Oscan House Books. I did cartwheels across her office." Juan sipped his soda before continuing. "Nancy wanted to have an attorney look it over before we decided whether or not to take it."

"Good advice."

"Might have been but shoot, that contract had so many zeros on it, I told Nancy— and I quote— 'I don't care if this contract makes me Lucifer's personal valet, I'm signing this sucker.'" Juan chuckled before he flipped the Pepsi back to his mouth.

Bodie gave a faint smile. "And so it began," he said quietly.

"Basically." Juan nodded.

Not breaking eye contact, Bodie lifted his glass and held it outstretched. "Cheers."

Juan's smile stayed in place as he lifted his soda. "Cheers," he repeated before clinking it with his own.

Tab McGrifth

14

"Tab, you know that first story you covered? The one dealing with the rape?" Whitey rasped.

Tab scratched his head as he moved his mind back in time. "Yep. It was the rape of that gal by that Black man."

"That's the one." Whitey nodded and took a sip of his Jack. "You can imagine my surprise when I heard Ms. Ida Lee's voice coming from the radio."

Ms. Ida Lee. She had been at WDMN so long that you could almost mistake her for a fixture. Her gray bun, dresses up to her neck and wrinkles from her head to her ying yang didn't help her out either. Tab hadn't thought of her in years.

"There I was at the Country Club and they had the station playing full blast and Ms. Ida Lee's whiny voice comes on to announce the next song. I was fit to be tied right there. I didn't know what the hell was going on." Whitey chuckled.

"So you told me. I remember I was playing a round of Quartet songs and somebody ran into the station and yelled that a white girl had been raped. Then they said it was by a Black man. Actually, he said Colored, but I tell you, my head almost flew off my neck!" Tab stated indignantly. "A white gal raped by a Black man? Oh, that was a pure travesty!"

Whitey leaned back into his chair. "So you got Ida Lee to spin the records and—"

"Not so fast. At first I didn't know what to do. Folks was running in and out so fast with more tidbits of news, my head started to swim."

"I guess Ms. Ida Lee was pretty upset, too." Whitey smirked.

"Yes, indeedy. She said she knew that poor gal and couldn't imagine which one of our Coloreds could have done it." Tab shook his head as if to say, 'Dumb broad.'

"So what happened next?"

"I couldn't let news of this magnitude pass me by so I made a decision. I was gonna cover the story and put it on the radio so we could ferret out that varmint and deal with him as quickly as possible. Even though Ms. Ida Lee was sniffing, I told her she had to man the record player while I found out what was going on."

"What did she say to that?" Whitey held out his glass for another shot of whiskey. Tab poured it before he answered.

"Oh, you know how women are—'I can't do that' and stuff. I shushed her and showed her how to put the record on then push the button before she announced what was playing." He pantomimed his actions.

"That simple, huh?"

"Yes. A woman likes a man in control." Tab winked.

Whitey guffawed "True. Ida Mae probably hadn't seen that in a while since her Wilbert was a weakling. He would run if he saw his shadow. I don't know why she wasted all those years on him anyway," Whitey groused.

"Me neither, but she put the records on like I showed her and I went out to get the news." Tab sipped his beer before continuing. "At first, folks just had a bunch of speculations. Then somebody said the girl—I can't remember her name to save my life—anyway, they said the girl had named her attacker. Jeremiah Mosh…Moose..."

"Jebediah Moses. His name was Jebediah Moses," Whitey finished for him. "I was surprised when I heard that myself. The Moses' were quiet, respectable Coloreds."

"That's what everybody thought until they heard about what he'd done to that gal. Tore her up good, they say." Tab grimaced.

Whitey shook his head in silence.

"So once I heard the name, I got to the phone in Grant's Drugstore and called back to the station on the request line. I told Ms. Ida Lee what to do so I could be on live. Then I started talking. I interviewed everybody around me—you know they were excited to be on the radio—and then I urged the good, Christian citizens to find the scalawag so we could deal with him." He pointed his finger at Whitey.

"By the time I reached the station, there must have been a thousand folks crowded around doorways, trying to hear what you were saying on the radio."

"I know it. It got so noisy in the drugstore, I told Fred to let me use the extension in the back room."

"So that's where you had gotten off to. I was trying to locate you but nobody knew where you had gone."

"That's where I was—waging war in the storage room. I talked about how the Coloreds always lusted after our women and how sinful it was. How if we let this type of thing go on, no telling how many of our women would be accosted by them. We *had* to find the varmint."

"They found him, all right. They say he was at home, just about to sit down to supper." Whitey sucked at his dentures before digging into the back of his mouth.

"Eating and he just raped a white woman. No conscience at all." Tab shook his head in disgust. "I liked to have jumped for joy when Fred stuck his head in and told me the Sheriff was escorting him to the jail."

"You know, the folks threw rocks at him and tried to tear him away from the deputies, but they held him strong. Yep, those deputies made a few enemies that day. Especially with the folks they hit with clubs." Whitey sucked at some remnant of food on his finger.

Tab looked away, hiding his repulsion. "Damn shame they had to hit our good, Christian folks like that. Afterall, they were just exercising their right to bear arms."

"Matter of opinion there, but go on." Whitey waved his hand.

"Well, I announced that they had Jebediah and pleaded for all the good folks to come down and voice their displeasure. And they did. In droves." Tab paused. "Before long, I moved back to the front of the store to keep all the action in view since everyone was outside."

"You saw when they stormed the jailhouse?"

"Yessireebob. I was standing on a stool, yelling into that phone. I could hear my voice coming out of all the radios and I was psyched! Hell, I was making a difference! All those people would never have known what was happening if it hadn't been for me." He pointed at his puffed chest.

"Yep. That's true. The station got a big boost when the big time radio outlets up North got a hold of that blow-by-blow tape." Whitey nodded then gave him a penetrating stare. "So do you feel bad about what they did to Jebediah?"

"A rapist? You've got to be kidding me." Tab folded his arms across his chest and arched his eyebrow. "When they pulled that coon out of the building and threw that rope around the oak tree in the courtyard, I was elated. That's the way justice is supposed to work. Swift. I tell you, I didn't stop talking until I saw the last jerks from that coon's body." He punctuated the air with his finger. "By that time, I was hoarse and drained."

"Ahem." Whitey looked at him closely. "You know that girl? The one that supposedly got raped?"

Tab stiffened. "Why do you say 'supposedly'? They said her husband found her just after it happened. Her clothes were off and juice was running down her legs. No supposedly in that," Tab finished, confidence radiating from his eyes.

Whitey scrunched his face. "Now Tab, that gal was…loose. Hell, half the town had been up in her cooze, including *me*, and you telling me some Colored man's got to rape her to get what she gives out freely? A man out of a good family? You ever see his wife?"

"No."

"Well, she was a looker. I mean Lena Horne kind of looker. That gal that supposedly got raped looked a hell of a sight worse that she did. Think! Why would a man that has caviar at home be sniffing up behind some rotten egg out in the street?" Whitey whipped his hand through his sparse hair. "I'll bet it wasn't Jebediah Moses at all. That gal had probably been letting somebody sample her honey and her husband came back before she could get herself cleaned up so she screamed 'Rape!' to cover her ass."

They had found their man and now, years later Whitey is saying it wasn't so? Tab refused to consider this. He chose his words carefully. "Just because she fooled around and was from the wrong side of town doesn't mean she shouldn't be respected. Hell, she was a White woman, not some Jew or Dago. Coloreds having sex with White women is a sin. It says so in the Bible."

"You sure that's what it says?"

"I sure am. Besides, even if Jebediah didn't do it, some other Colored did—" Whitey threw his hands in the air and rolled his eyes at the ceiling, "—so I guess that's the one who should be feeling bad about the whole situation. If he'd just kept his pecker in his pants, another one of his kind would still be alive."

"That was a ballsy call you made by fingering the man on speculation alone. It could have blown up in all our faces. Hell, it nearly did when the NAACP got involved."

The NAACP had reacted swiftly. The blacks had marched and chanted and written every congressman who was partial to their bullshit. "But it didn't. Tough times call for tough decisions. The girl called his name so it wasn't speculation, it was fact. I made the decision and live with it. Gladly." Tab smiled.

Whitey sniffed the air as if it were foul. "I sure hope so."

"I do."

Whitey looked at the puffed up chest and smirked before he asked the next question. "Well then, since you feel that-a-way," he paused for effect, "tell me about Rosaparks Simpson."

Tab's curse reverberated around the room.

Deva

15

"You want a drink or something?" Ed inquired.

Deva shook her head. "I don't drink unless it's something I've brought myself."

"Good policy. I imagine there are a lot of crazies that wouldn't mind slipping you a 'Roofie' and having their way with you." He winked and leered.

Deva didn't find any humor in the statement. She'd had encounters with some 'crazies' and was well aware of what they could and would do if they had the opportunity. She pulled her shawl tighter. "I'm glad you can joke about it, but it's a scary reality for me."

The smile left Ed's face. "Hey, I didn't mean to sound so insensitive. I guess it's just that sometimes I forget what precautions you have to take being famous and all." He looked at Jarrel sitting by the fire.

Deva followed his eyes before replying. "Yeah. It's no longer just living life footloose and fancy-free. I've got to be careful about each little detail. One mistake could cost me everything…even my life." She thought about the murdered actor again.

"I hear you." Ed nodded. Seeing her unease, he changed the subject. "You know, I noticed that your singing style has changed over the last two albums. On your first one, you sung songs like we used to sing."

Deva snorted. "And almost lost my shirt in the process."

"What do you mean?" Ed questioned. "Hell, we sounded good."

"The songs on that first album were hand-picked by the record company. I wasn't really feeling some of them, but I was so elated with the contract, I went ahead with them against my better judgment." Deva rolled her eyes to the ceiling. "Big mistake. I think we barely sold fifty thousand copies. We wouldn't have sold those if I hadn't done a college tour."

"I'm sorry to hear that. I really dug that album." Ed shifted in his seat. "You looked so like...*you* on the cover."

"Who do I look like now?" Deva squawked.

"You look like you except...souped up."

"Don't start that war paint mess again," Deva wailed.

Ed held up his hands. "I won't. I'm just saying your look has changed. Heck, even your videos changed. I remember the one for *Inside My Head.* You seemed so innocent. Fresh." Ed smiled at the memory.

"That was another record company decision. They wanted me to look like a scrubbed-clean, girl-next-door. But I knew that wasn't going to be enough, not with all the competition out there. People might like the voice, but the video *sells* the record."

"That's hard to believe. Your voice is so incredible. It's gotten stronger, better."

Deva looked at him in surprise. "You think so, too?" Ed agreed. "It seemed like once I signed the contract with Hans, my voice just peaked. No coaching or anything. Sometimes I'm shocked at how great I sound even after touring for months."

"Well, whatever you're doing, don't change 'cause your pipes are raising the roof!" Ed held up a hand for a high-five which Deva gave with relish.

"Thankya. Thankya."

"I'm serious. When you sang *Finally Yours,* you made the hairs stand up on my body." Ed shivered. "I've never heard anything like the high notes you hit at the end."

Deva giggled. "That was pure improvisation on my part. I thought the song needed…something. Some *shazaam!* you know? So when I reached the end, the scatting just came out on its own. I guess my brain acted on my subconscious thoughts and directed my vocal chords all by itself." Deva flipped her hand into the air.

"It was beautiful, no matter who was running the show."

"I thought it would be nominated for a Grammy, but no potatoes."

"Damn shame. You sound as good as, if not better, than Beyonce' or Christina."

"Maybe, but I still didn't get nominated."

"*That* year."

"Yeah. That all changed with the second album."

Ed frowned. "Everything changed with the second album."

Deva tsked. "Don't be like that. I knew I had to step up to the plate, so I did what needed to be done."

"But so many changes. Your look. Your videos." He twisted his lips.

"Hey, it's been worth the changes. True, my mother just about had a stroke with the *Drop the Booty* video, but that album went platinum in two weeks flat." Deva snapped her fingers.

"No you didn't mention *that* video. Ghettofabulous at its zenith! At first, I was wondering who in the world this chick was wiggling like that on the video. Then I just about had a stroke when I saw your name in the credits."

Deva whooped. "Who didn't? My cell phone was like the hot line after that video dropped. I caught flack from a bunch of folks, especially newspapers and people from home."

"I'll bet. *I* didn't even recognize you and I've known you since forever. Girl, you hardly had any clothes on." Ed squinted and shook his head. "And the way you *worked* your hips…every man watching got a hard-on."

Deva grinned widely. "That was the point. Make folks horny enough to buy the album."

"Sure made folks do that."

"Ah huh. Ed, honey, sex sells. That was the beginning of my gravy train there. Albums flying off the shelves, magazines, radio and television stations begging me for interviews…I was on Cloud Nine."

"I can imagine," Ed said then leaned his elbow on the table. "Do you know how many girls started dressing like you?"

"Millions. That's why I launched my own line," Deva retorted.

"Millions of nearly naked chicks walking the streets from watching a video. Sometimes when I see these girls, I just have to shake my head. They don't leave anything to the imagination. Hell, it's all there for the world to see. It's to the point where they're half-naked even in the winter. Just sad." Ed's mouth turned down.

"Hey, I'm not always half-naked. Look at me now." She motioned at her attire.

"Yeah, but those girls don't see you like this. They see you in the videos and on billboards and television. *Then* you barely have enough to cover the 'essentials.'" Ed quoted with his fingers.

"Essentials are in the eye of the beholder. Besides, I think they all looked tasteful."

"Yeah. I guess you think the boob-pasty-half-your-butt-exposed thing you wore to the Grammy's last year was tasteful." Ed cocked an eyebrow.

Deva had created a sensational buzz with her designer dress that had no top to one side with only a plastic flower covering the nipple of the exposed breast. The back was just as scandalous, extending down to the indention in her hips. She was the topic of numerous conversations—no, make that arguments—on television, radio and in magazines and newspapers.

"Baby, y'all ain't seen nothing yet!"

Ed rolled his head around in feigned disgust. "Girl, you are a mess!"

"Am not!"

"Yes, you are. And since I'm asking, I might as well ask this: What in hell were you thinking when you tongued Maiden down on that stage?"

Deva screamed in laughter before falling back in the chair, hands clutching at her sides.

Juan Rodriguez

16

"So, how do you deal with the heat from the Fag Patrol?" Bodie asked, scratching at his face.

"Fag Patrol?" Juan was puzzled. He was aware of most of the Gay/Lesbian organizations but this was a new one for him.

"Yeah. The reporters and radio commentators who give you crap about your writing."

"Oh. To be honest, the more they talk about me, the more books I sell."

Bodie laughed long and hard. "Bet they don't realize that, do they?"

"I'd say not. Otherwise, they'd leave me alone. I don't plan to tell them either. *See Me for Me* is in its fifth printing and going strong. *Two Daddies* is on its second, so let them talk. I'm laughing all the way to the bank." Juan shrugged.

"You'd think after all these years, they would just leave gay folks alone."

Juan shook his head. "Naw. We're different. People are always afraid of differences."

"But we really aren't. We want the same things that straight folks want—love, money and power."

"Yeah, but we *chose* to love someone of the same sex."

Bodie propped an elbow on the table, jutted his chin out. "And they *chose* to love someone of the opposite sex."

"Therein lies the controversy. They think of gayness as a disease that's highly contagious. Afraid it will infect little Johnny or Joanne." Juan had had this discussion before and it always ended in a stalemate.

"They make me want to puke with that crap. Most gays don't try to *turn* anybody," Bodie sneered. "They want people who want the same thing they are looking for. It's too hard to make someone fit the mold. Instead, we look for folks already molded."

"Hey, I'm convinced. Now tell that to the paranoid straight folks out there."

"You beat me to it with your book. I wish the dumbasses would read it."

Juan eyes crinkled at the corners. "Yeah, I did, didn't I?"

"Did you see the article where they tried to tie you into the child pornography thing?" Bodie bopped his head. "What am I saying? Of course you did. That stuff was too big to miss."

Juan stiffened. "You bet. Nancy was on that reporter at *The Daily Shout* like ants at a picnic. She demanded a retraction of that dribble immediately."

"She did? I didn't hear about that." Bodie licked at the foam around his mouth.

"You never do. The retractions are always in small print in some obscure portion of the paper, usually just before the Classifieds. The papers are careful to avoid letting people see they were wrong. It's bad for sales."

"Classic capitalism."

"It didn't help that someone hacked into my website and placed some kiddie nudes on there."

Bodie sat upright then let out a shrill whistle.

"You can say that again. The police even got involved. My nuts were in a wringer!" Juan's face scrunched at the recollection.

"You ever find out who did it?"

"The best answer they came up with was some university students pranking."

"That's a serious prank. You do some *long* time for child pornography these days." Bodie held his arms wide.

"Tell me about it. I had to spend nearly one hundred thou to prove my innocence. Those cops were ready to put my gay behind under the jail."

"Dude, I'm glad you got out of that."

"Me too. It seemed like just as the photos surfaced, the article dropped. The crap sprayed out of the fan. I had so many people hitting the website, it crashed."

Bodie squinted. "Ouch."

"Can you believe that I had three hundred thousand hits in one day? That's almost three every second of the day."

Bodie slapped his thigh. "The Pamela and Tommy Lee video site didn't get that many."

"And I didn't even have a video. The hackers only posted photos."

"Guess 'Inquiring Minds' were disappointed."

"Not too much. I sold one hundred thousand books in one week." Juan answered smugly.

"Didn't you have to sue another publication? I thought I read about you receiving a good chunk of money when they settled."

Juan ran aggravated fingers over his face. "Yeah, we did. That was *Out Today*. Can you believe they call themselves a 'Fag Rag'?"

"Are they the ones always trying to label this star or that one as the latest in-the-closet-sister?"

"One and the same. I don't know why they seem to hate my writing, though. I'm already out of the closet. If anything, I thought they'd be super-supportive."

"Well, all your sisters aren't *really* your sisters," Bodie said pointedly.

"Maybe, but to insinuate that I'd had a series of parties where I initiated a bunch of kids into the gay lifestyle was a bit much."

"I agree. Do you think that reporter was straight?"

"Had to be. The way that article was skewed, you'd have thought I was the leader of some gay cult. 'Children of the Gay Corn' or something they said. Anyway, I don't even know where that type of rumor could have started. Shit! I've *always* been monogamous." The fire in Juan's eyes dared Bodie to dispute him.

Bodie heard the hardness in his voice. Saw the fire in his eyes. He cleared his throat before he said, "Well, I can certainly vouch for you there."

"You should," Juan viciously crumpled the can and slammed it on the table, "after all the hell you put me through!"

Tab McGrifth

17

"Why the hell did you have to bring up *that* woman's name?" Tab said, jaw tight in anger.

"Hell, why not? She said you raped her and she's *Black* so I want to know what really happened." Whitey tilted his head, eyes glinting in amusement, as he waited for Tab's response.

"That bitch cost me a lot of time and money with her accusations is what happened!" Tab spat out.

"So I heard. Somewhere in the neighborhood of a cool million, wasn't it?"

"One point five, if you must know." Tab wrinkled his nose. "All to shut down a bunch of lies that slut put together."

"Now, Tab, the info I got was that you were looking at some real time. My source," Whitey drawled the word, "said they had enough evidence to convict you of at least sexual battery. Something about a dress with your seed plastered down the front of it. Don't worry. I ain't even gonna *ask* how that happened," Whitey wheezed out before a coughing spell hit him.

Tab remained silent. The flush on his face was evident even in the dim light.

"So what you got to say for yourself, boy?" Whitey asked between slurps of his whiskey.

Tab sat impassive. Through clenched teeth, he snarled, "I *don't* want to talk about it."

"Now, don't be that-a-way. I ain't passing judgment, I'm just yanking your chain. Hell, I've been up in every type of cooze on this earth and I gotta tell ya…it all feels the same in the dark!" Saliva sprayed from Whitey's mouth.

Tab's eyes burned in his head. "You don't know what you're talking about so shut the hell up!"

Whitey held a hand in front of him. "Hold up. Get your goddamn BVD's outta your crack. I'm just trying to point out the *irony* of you causing a Black man to get lynched for *supposedly* sleeping with a White gal and years later you do the same thing, only in reverse." Whitey leaned forward, his eyes demonic appearing in the light of the fire. Maniacal laughter bubbled from his throat as he spoke. "Don't seem like getting poontang is a hanging offense now, does it?"

Tab gripped the edge of the table—trying valiantly to push down the urge to slap the old fart in his mouth—as his wild laughter taunted him.

Deva

18

"You saw that, huh?" Deva gasped, hands holding her sides tight.

"Who didn't?" Ed grumbled. "There I am with a room full of folks, proudly giving 'shout outs' to my homegirl…then, you French-kiss Maydin on national TV like she was the best thing since air." Ed shook his head. "I could have dropped through the floor."

"It wasn't *that* bad," she protested.

"It was. Never in a million years would I have thought I would see something like that from you," Ed accused.

"Hey, it was a publicity stunt. Nothing more."

"Really." Ed looked unconvinced.

"Really. My promo guy thought that it would be a great way to boost record sales for both Maydin and myself since we both had albums out."

"Did it?"

"Did it what?"

"Boost sales."

"Though the damn roof. That album hit number one and stayed there for five months. My next one entered at number three. So it worked for me." Deva gave a 'thumbs up' sign.

"But, think…you are a role model."

"And?"

"And millions of girls, and guys, watch your every move, your dress and repeat your words. Now how do you think that kiss affected them?"

"Hey, kids are way more educated in the ways of sex than when we were coming up. They already experiment with stuff I still haven't done so I don't think they were swayed one way or the other."

"You know that's a lie," Ed said, eyes flashing. "They might be experimenting, but the reason they're experimenting so much is because the shit is everywhere. They're desensitized from what they see and hear everyday on television, movies, videos and music. They think it's normal behavior 'cause that's what's being shoved down their throats twenty-four-seven."

His soapbox diatribe irritated Deva. "What are you now? A preacher?"

"No, I haven't been called up to preach yet, but you don't have to be a preacher to know the truth."

"Your truth," Deva sneered.

"No, the truth. I'm concerned about how seeing two women kissing on a show that millions of *families* watched affected the kids. It gave a thumbs up to homosexuality."

"It did not. I don't think seeing two women kissing would ever cause a person to become gay. Either they are or they aren't."

"So you don't think the constant brain-washing of easy sex and violence hasn't caused kids to do some things they might not otherwise have considered either?"

"Oh, *please.*" Deva waved the question away. "I see the mess all the time and I don't act any differently than I ever did. My values are still the same small town ones I've always had. Don't let the exterior fool you." She gave him a pointed look.

"Girl, what rock you been living under? Most kids aren't being raised like we were. They don't have two good parents showing them right from wrong. The majority are raised in one-parent households and spend a bunch of time unsupervised. That's one of the reasons juvenile delinquency is on the rise."

"The rate is on the rise because these chaps are bad as hell," Deva asserted.

"*Because* they have a lot of free, no-parent time on their hands. Don't you remember all the crap we used to do when our folks were away from home?"

Deva did. She and Ed spent plenty of time devising new and improved ways of making mischief. To be honest, if they did some of the stuff they'd done back then now, they would be in jail. She softened. "Yeah, I do. But even though we did them, we knew right from wrong."

"But a lot of these kids don't. They raise themselves based on what they see on television."

"I still don't buy that. They aren't like us. This generation is a new breed with a bunch of ingrained misconceptions."

"Perpetuated by the media and their role models," Ed countered. "How else do you explain why the majority of Black boys want to be rap stars and young girls look like hookers in high school?"

"Got dropped on their head at birth?" Deva gave Ed a wide eye look.

"Some, but not that many. There wouldn't be a practicing OB-GYN if that were true." Ed laughed.

"Yeah, but there would be a bunch of wealthy families from the settlements." Deva giggled at the thought. As their laughter slowed, she leaned forward and perused him for a long moment.

"What?" Ed finally asked, uneasy with the way she was watching him.

"Since I'm the downfall of the nations kids, I was just wondering when you were going to get around to asking the 'Big Question.' "

"What?" Ed squinted at her in confusion.

Deva paused for effect. She smiled slyly before she said, "About the 'wardrobe malfunction' at the Superball half-time."

Ed slapped his hands over his face and groaned loudly.

19

Bodie took another swallow from his beer before slowly returning it to the table. He ran his hands through his hair, tugging at the roots before he spoke. "Still upset, huh?"

"Yes," Juan answered tightly.

Bodie rocked his body while staring at Juan. "You know, man, it wasn't personal."

"It was to *me*." Juan tapped his chest.

"I can see how you'd think that but I swear it wasn't. It was just…I was going through some things."

"Yeah, a bunch of young, hot asses."

The remark stung, but Bodie let it pass. "I loved you. Hell, I still do."

Juan didn't need to hear this. "Stop. Please. You don't love anyone but you."

"That's not fair. All the time we were together I tried to shower you with all the love I was capable of giving."

"You mean willing to carve out for me. Your other boy-toys got the rest."

"Hey—"

"Wait a minute! I'm not through talking." Juan sighed deeply, fingers vigorously rubbing the beads in his pocket. "When I walked in on you while your lap was fused to that dude's ass, I died. Literally." Bodie opened his mouth to speak but Juan held up a finger and stopped him. "Everything was suddenly a lie. An obese, ugly, preposterous lie invented by the man I loved unconditionally. I was willing to lay down and *die* for you. And you saw fit to take all that love and squash it under your feet like *trash*."

Juan's words were brutal but Bodie was a man of experience. If he didn't know anything else, he *knew* men. Especially the men that had loved him at one time or another. No discomfiture was present in his voice when he spoke. "Juan, God knows I hurt you. I didn't mean to…but that's the way it turned out."

"You did more than just 'hurt me.' You devastated me. I wanted to kill myself from the heartache and pain."

"I know what I did was way past wrong and no apology will do to change that. But no matter how things went down, I loved you. Hell, truth be told, I was scared of how I was feeling." Bodie slid a honeyed smile onto his lips. "I mean, I was the older man and suddenly I find myself head-over-heels in love with a kid? I couldn't deal with it. I was trying to convince myself that I didn't need you. That you could be replaced."

"Did it work?"

"No." Bodie covered Juan's unmoving hand, his voice dropping to just above a whisper. "I've got to confess…I've *never* loved a man the way I loved you."

This statement made Juan's fingers manipulate the beads faster.

"You didn't know that, huh?"

"No. I didn't." Juan contemplated whether Bodie's love confession would have made any difference if he'd known. Would he have tried to work it out? Or would the outcome have been the same? Bodie interrupted his thought pattern.

"I can see this information has thrown you for a loop." Bodie removed his hand and leaned back into the chair.

"Yeah…it has." Juan hoped Bodie had no idea of how much it had.

"Well, let's talk about something else for a minute." A ghost of a smile played around Bodie's mouth. "You know, the same-sex marriage stance you made has really solidified our community."

Ever since the same-sex marriage argument made it to the forefront of America's 'reality check' meter, Juan had made it a point to promote it as much as he could. It was his belief that marriage didn't just mean man-woman. It could and should mean two committed, monogamous partners willing to do whatever was needed to have a solid relationship. One that could stand the test of time. He felt he had reached that particular place in life—enough money, age and wisdom—where other opinions didn't matter when one needed to take a stand.

He'd gone on a media blitz—commercials, full-page newspaper and magazine ads, as well as the radio circuit—telling anyone who would listen his views. At first, there was a backlash. His books sales plummeted and vocal opposition was loud and boisterous. But as is normal, the Sisterhood closed ranks and the grass-roots effort regained momentum. The state and federal Supreme Courts were petitioned relentlessly. It paid off. Massachusetts was set to be the initiation grounds for the first of the marriages. If the movement was successful there, the rest of the nation would follow suit…That was the general consensus anyway.

"You mean started a mess of shit, don't you?" Juan laughed, feeling on more comfortable ground.

"That was to be expected, especially with such a controversial subject as man-man/woman-woman marriage. The good old American people weren't ready to deal with it. It was all right as long as we stayed in our place, but when it's put out there where you can't deny it…it rubs your thighs pretty raw."

"Some folks wanted to personally rub some other parts of me raw along with the thighs."

"I'll bet. Did you get any hate mail?"

"Did I get any? You mean, how much did I get? The post office called and told me they were going to assess me a delivery fee because of all the mail I was getting. Hell, I couldn't even send an email since my box was clogged all the time."

"Guess them remembering the website incident didn't help."

"Not one damn bit. But this is something I feel strongly about. Two *people*—doesn't matter who's paired with whom—who love each other should have the opportunity to see how far that love can take them. It shouldn't be up to some court to decide whether or not they will allow me to feel for someone or sex them up like the next person. Let my unique relationship grow just like any other one."

"And government be damned!"

"Right. Government be damned."

"So why haven't you signed up to get married yet?"

"Truth is, I'm thinking about it...but..." Juan's voice trailed off in...*doubt?*

Bodie's heartbeat surged. "You know, dude, that's the main reason I needed to see you again." Bodie giggled nervously. "The fact of the matter is...I want us to get back together."

That news slammed into Juan like a sack of cement. "Wha...what?"

"Yeah. I want you back, man. Forever." Bodie rummaged around in his jacket pocket before extracting a small box. He held it out for Juan to take. "Open it."

This was way more than Juan had bargained for. All the words he'd wanted to hear were now being spoken...except the timing was wrong. Bodie was all wrong. His hand remained on the table. "Bodie, what's in the box?" he asked, already knowing what few things could be concealed in a two by two square box.

"Open it up and see for yourself," Bodie urged, sweat glistening on his brow.

"No. You tell me."

Bodie didn't say anything, just opened the box for Juan to see for himself. A wide, platinum wedding band stared up at him, winking with promises for the future.

Juan couldn't have spoken if his life depended on it.

Tab McGrifth

20

"Whitey, what did you want to tell me?" Tab asked somberly. This meeting had gone way different from what he'd envisioned and he was past ready to get out of there.

Whitey waved his question away. "We gonna get to that. Right now I just want to ruminate on your career a bit. Hell, it's been years since we had a chance to sit and gab our jaws a spell." His old man jowls jiggled in concert with his arm movements.

That was true, but despite this fact, if Whitey brought up any more bullshit episodes, Tab was leaving and that was that. "All right. What else you been remembering?"

"You know, I heard your broadcast about Newjean Boudreax just before they executed him."

Tab smiled. Newjean Boudreax was a sixteen-year-old Cajun convicted of murdering his mother and stepfather. Though he'd repeatedly said his stepfather had molested him for years, Tab didn't believe that dribble one bit. Hell, he knew the Boudreaxs. They were members of his country club and upstanding citizens. They had the looks, money and a big house with maids waiting on them hand and foot. Tom and his wife, Marjorie, were the perfect couple. Then his stepson kills them. Swore Tom Boudreaux was raping him daily and his mother refused to stop him. He'd killed them in self-defense, not malice.

Despite the medical doctor's reports indicating that Newjean had been repeatedly sodomized, the teenager was convicted of capital murder and sentenced to die. A bunch of civil liberty groups got into the fray begging for a retrial, conversion of his sentence or clemency. It seemed like they were making some headway when the governor announced he would investigate the case personally. That's when Tab jumped into the fracas.

To let a convicted murderer get less than he deserved was a slap in the face to the justice system, even if he was only sixteen. Hell, who said kids should get a second chance at anything in life? That Newjean stood to inherit everything in the wake of his parent's deaths fueled this conviction.

Tab took to the airways and let his opinions fly. He'd invited rebuttal medical experts and child psychologists who agreed with him. On the sly, Tab took a trip to the governor's mansion to discuss the ramifications of any show of leniency on this issue. It seemed to have worked. The governor shut his trap and Newjean went down in history as the youngest person ever executed in recent memory.

Tab slapped a self-satisfied grin on his face. "That was some of the best editorial work I've ever done."

"Sure was some piece of work," Whitey spat.

"Yep, it was," Tab answered proudly, ignoring Whitey's tone. "That Newjean had some 'evil juju' in him. To just kill your parent's in cold blood like that...you know he was already rotten to the core."

Whitey wrinkled up his face. "You don't think the boy was really being porked up the ass like he claimed?"

"Naw. Hell, he was looking for any way to save his skinny butt. Tom wasn't no faggot."

"How do you know he *wadn't* for sure? Plenty of folks act one way in public and the story is way, way, way different behind closed doors. Think about how many times we've seen or heard about 'prominent citizens' beating the hell out of their spouses and molesting their kids. What made Tom any different than those folks?" Whitey questioned.

"Well, for one, I knew Tom and Marjorie. Two, I knew that snot-nosed Newjean. He was always the one causing trouble at the country club. In fact, he managed to almost get the Boudreax's membership revoked with his pissing in the pool stunt. They had to do plenty of brown-nosing to keep it. Hell, I knew it was a matter of time before he brought them some serious grief," Tab stated righteously.

"Maybe the boy was acting out his frustrations. Being your daddy's punk-ass has got to melt some of those brain cells; make you feel like you're not a boy."

Tab dismissed his argument. "Please. That punk was just a spoiled rotten kid. He sassed them constantly. Just disrespectful. I'm telling you, Tom had his hands full with that little bastard."

"So you think the doctor's were lying about him being buggered, too? Some kind of conspiracy to save Newjean even at the risk of perjury?"

"Personally, I think the boy was already taking it up the pooper-shooter...by choice. It wasn't Tom reaming him out, it was his own friends."

"So he murdered his parents without any known motive and used his extracurricular activities as an alibi?" Whitey gave him an I-don't-believe-you-believe-that-shit look.

Tab plowed forward, angry at his implication. "He *tried.* Thankfully, the good folks saw through that mess and gave him what he deserved."

"Neal Burris seemed set on converting his sentence at one time. What happened with that?"

Tab laughed long and hard. "I had a 'private talk' with Governor Burris. Helped him see the error of his thinking."

"Don't tell me you squeezed out 'ol Burris! He ran as the straight-arrow candidate. I didn't think he would bow to pressure like that."

"Goes to show you all arrows don't fly straight, don't it?"

"Yup. But don't you think that him dying at eighteen was a pure waste of a life? He could have been given a juvenile sentence, been rehabilitated and then gotten back to pulling his weight in society."

Tab gave Whitey a once-over before he answered. "Whitey, when did you get converted 'cause the old Whitey I know would *never* of said something like that."

Whitey shrugged his shoulders. "You live and you learn. Wasting a life just to make a point don't set right with me no more. I could see if he was an adult and knew better, but teenagers don't think like you and me. They don't weigh out the consequences to their actions."

Tab hit the table with his fist. "Pshaw! That twerp thought enough to plan how he was gonna blow their brains out, didn't he? That right there should show you that age don't matter when you're a killer! Young or old, they all deserve the same thing. Death."

Whitey twirled his cup between thumb and forefinger; sloshed the minimal fluid around in the bottom before he spoke again. "You got to be careful at how you judge folks so quick. We didn't walk not an inch in that boy's shoes so we don't know for sure if he was lying or telling the truth. From all accounts, I'd have given him the benefit of the doubt." His words were weighty in the air.

Tab looked at the sunken features and slumped shoulders of the man he'd once held high on his totem pole and shook his head in sorrow. "Well, I hope this doesn't sound too mean, but…I sure as hell am glad you weren't on that jury."

With that, Tab chugged his beer and gave a deep, satisfied sigh.

Deva

21

"Girl, what's happened to you? First, the video where you shake your booty like there's no tomorrow, then kissing a woman on stage, now this. What went through your mind when your PR guy thought this one up? I say PR guy 'cause I *know* you didn't cook this crap up on your own." Ed looked at her suspiciously.

"For your information, I thought up the idea…but things just went a little differently than I'd planned," Deva commented in a low voice and dropped her eyes.

Ed groaned again. "So you really did plan to have your boob exposed to the entire nation?"

"Well…not like that," Deva huffed and wrung her hands together.

"Then how?"

She blew a stream of air out of her mouth before answering. "When Jimmie Tomahawk and I cooked up the idea, he was supposed to just pull the outer layer off and I'd be covered with the red sheer silk. Boob visible but not *really* visible. You know, sensationalism. Somehow, though, we got caught up in the moment and he must have been remembering our fling and—"

"*Fling?* You and Jimmie Tomahawk had a fling?" Ed's mouth hung open. "Why, he's just a kid."

Jimmie Tomahawk was the latest teenage sensation. Good looks, buffed body and pipes to boot. When he first began flirting with Deva, she had brushed him off. With groupies in every shape and nationality lining her door after each appearance, what did she need with some lovestruck teenager? Yes, he was way different from the men that had been in her life recently with his clean cut look, but she didn't think he'd be any type of challenge. What teenager was to a grown young woman? She had real grown men available at the snap of her fingers.

But Jimmy Tomahawk had other plans. He wore puppy love eyes and sent unrelenting love notes asking for just one chance to spend an evening with her. He'd said he was convinced he had the tools to change her mind. Eventually he'd worn her down. She'd given in and been sorry that she had. Yes, he had the right bed moves and silky words but after that there was…open space. She needed more so she ended the relationship.

Deva had the good grace to look momentarily ashamed but then rebounded swiftly. "How old do you think I am? He's eighteen…I think…and I'm only twenty-three."

"But when did this fling happen?"

"A year ago. So?"

"Girl, they're gonna pick your narrow butt up! You're guilty of child molestation."

Deva whisked his comment away. "Am not. He was a willing participant. *Very* willing," she said with a wink.

"Who wouldn't be? Hell, sex with Deva has got to be one of the best situations for any man. He'd have been a fool to turn you down." Ed thought about how he'd wanted to take their relationship further and she'd rebuffed him then pushed the thought away as he felt the old anger creeping up his spine. "But why would he be mad about it and try to take it out on you like that?"

"I dumped him."

"Ouch. That must have hurt like hell to a young, upcoming stud like Jimmie." Ed silently gloated at his dismissal.

"You better believe it. His mother had the nerve to call me and cuss me out because she said I'd 'toyed with his affections' then dumped him like dog crap." Deva looked affronted.

"Did you?" A smile crinkled the corner of his eyes.

"Of course not. Our relationship had run its course. Jimmie is good to look at…but he just didn't stimulate me mentally."

"I'm sure he was concerned with stimulating some other parts of your anatomy besides your brain." Ed turned smoldering eyes towards her. Deva read the look and turned away. Sensing her discomfort, he focused back on the conversation. "OK, so go on. He was remembering y'all's fling and what happened?"

"Well, when he was singing that night, he seemed different than he'd been in rehearsals. More intense." Deva gave a confused shake of her head. "I don't know if you heard him, but he kept talking between his singing. Promised to 'strip me to my G-string by the end of this song' or something like that. I just discounted it as being caught up in the moment and that must have been the case, because when he hit the last note and grabbed my shirt like we'd practiced, he tugged a little too hard…and *BAM!* here comes the nipple."

"And you just *happened* to be wearing an intricate nipple ring in your boob that night."

"For your information, I always wear a nipple ring of some sort." Deva knew Ed would be mortified to know not only did she wear a nipple ring, the other nipple was also pierced along with her tongue, navel and clitoris.

"Seems like if you'd planned not to remove the entire covering, you'd have left it off. You know, just in case he caught on it by accident. I mean, he could have torn your nipple slap off your chest if the material had gotten wrapped around one of the edges or something."

Deva winced at the image. "Okay. It was a terrible idea, but I still didn't plan for it to go that far."

"Apparently he did. When you play with fire, you're bound to get burned."

"Tell me about it. In this instance, we both got burned. The FCC fined our tails like we were Midas' kids."

Ed slapped the table. "They had to do something. You brought nudity to Prime Time! They couldn't just sit back and twiddle their thumbs and say, 'Damn, did you see that? She's hot!' or some mess like that. They had to take action."

"But four hundred thousand is a bit much. It was an accident."

"An accident gone wrong, you mean. If you'd pulled it off, you wouldn't be saying this."

"True. But I have to admit, the furor made my album shoot to the sky. Sales doubled in the two weeks after the incident," Deva smoozed.

Ed swung his head from side to side. "Lenora, Lenora, Lenora. There's more to this thing we call 'life' than album sales."

"Maybe to you, but to me it means more cash, more vacations, more houses, more cars, more jewelry, more—"

"Stop," Ed interrupted her accelerating voice with upheld palms, "I get the picture. It's kind of sad to hear it from you, though. Even though money makes folks act a fool, I just didn't think you'd be part of the Fool's Choir."

"Please. Get a reality check." Deva rolled her eyes. "I don't care how much you'd like to believe that you're different from me, but you're not. If you don't have money, you're invisible."

"If you put your emphasis on self-respect, you'll always be visible, even if it's only to yourself," Ed retorted.

That argument didn't wash with Deva. "Yeah. Tell that to the proud, homeless man standing in the soup kitchen line wishing he had five dollars to buy his kids some bologna and bread. I'll bet his broke tail is full of self-respect," she retorted nastily.

"You're taking my words and mixing them up," Ed groused.

"No, I'm repeating what you said just like I heard it," she summed up.

"Then you misunderstood. I meant that money can buy a lot of things, external things, but money can never give you self-respect. Because no matter what exterior you present to the world, you know what being you truly are inside. If you respect yourself, everything is cool. If not, you do foolish things to gain attention to make sure they have the opportunity to *think* you're great. Just a façade."

Deva squared her back, lifted her chin. "Are you calling me a fake?" Challenging.

"No, but I think you've gotten so far away from who you once were, you think this is really the real you," he replied, not blinking.

"It is," she stated defiantly.

Ed glared at his childhood friend. You could smell the tension between them. He was very precise when he spoke again. "Lenora, you might be right, you might be wrong. But any way you toss a dog's ass, it still smells like shit."

Poison darts shot from Deva's eyes.

Juan Rodriguez

22

The silence was palpable as Juan stared at the ring. His fingers rubbed the plastic rosary vigorously. So much so, it was hot under his nimble fingers.

Bodie cleared his throat, a grin plastered on his face. "So what do you say? Want to get married?"

Juan couldn't believe him. His words. His actions. Why here? Now? He thought about Zeus and Loam. His family. His duo of love. There by his side over the past five years. Each day erasing the pain of Bodie—and other's Juan had wasted time on—from his heart. How Bodie could even fathom he could waltz in here and get back what they'd had just because *he* wanted to scratched at his psyche. *Did he really have the gall to believe he held that type of power over him? Still?*

Juan was outraged at Bodie, but more so at himself for allowing him the opportunity to get back under his skin. With anger coursing through his veins, he slapped the offending box from Bodie's hand. It tip-toed across the table before tumbling off the edge.

"Hey! What's wrong with you?" Bodie slid the chair back and reached towards the floor.

Juan felt an irascible urge to kick him in the face for playing him like a sucker. "You know what the fuck is wrong with me!" A dribble of saliva collected on his bottom lip. "How dare you try some shit like this with me!"

Bodie drew back from the barrage of words. "What a minute, man. I'm not playing some game. I want you back! For real!"

Though Juan heard the earnest tone of voice, he was past the point of being convinced. "Like hell you do! If that was so, you'd have looked me up a long time ago."

"I just told you I only recently realized this."

" 'You only recently realized this' " Juan mimicked nastily. "So you think since you've finally come to your senses, I should hop and be grateful and we'll ride off into the sunset happily fucking ever after?" He felt bile rising in his throat. "You've got some damn nerve."

Bodie perched on the edge of his chair watching for any sudden moves from Juan. He'd known his pronouncement would bring a visceral reaction…however, he hadn't planned on his reaction being so negative. So much for Plans A, B and C. They had definitely zoomed to X, Y or Z instead.

Bodie changed tactics. His eyes watered and lips trembled. He sniffed before he spoke quietly. "But you always said you wanted to marry me. Now we've got the chance."

Juan gave him a disgusted look. "What the hell did I know? I was just a green-assed kid, blinded by your love. Or rather lust. Because people in love don't treat their partners like you did."

" 'The people you love always hurt you the most.' " Bodie quoted an old, and in Juan's opinion, tired assed cliché.

"Say it again, Sam," Juan growled.

"But that was the old Bodie. I'm through with the love shuffle. I want monogamy. The *one* partner to share my ups and downs. To take care of me when I'm sick. To bask in the glow of our accomplishments. To grow old with," Bodie pleaded.

Juan ignored the pleading voice and eyes. "And what am I supposed to do about Zeus? And Loam? Just send Zeus a 'Dear John' letter thanking him for his participation however his services will no longer be necessary?"

A flush spread upwards from Bodie's neckline.

"Should I tell Loam 'Hey, buddie, now you've got three daddies instead of two,' and mess his head up? Tear apart the only family he's ever known...so you and I can do the vertical tango again? Should I?" Juan pushed.

"It's not like—"

"Like what?" Juan snarled, a pulse jumping in his temple. "It's exactly what you hoped I'd do. Run back into your waiting arms. Exit *them*. Enter you." He stood, shifted back his chair. "I'm outta here."

"Wait!" Bodie stood and held his hands on Juan's chest, not caring they were creating a scene.

Juan slapped the hands down. "Get the hell out of my way!" he yelled, stepping around the table.

Bodie pushed into the moving body. "No, wait!" Juan stopped, his eyes boring into Bodie's skull. "There are some...things I need to...say. *Important* things...that need to be said here." He dragged his hand through his mane. "Can we sit down?"

Juan stood, body tensed for battle.

"Please. Let's sit down." Bodie giggled nervously. "Folks are staring at us." Juan looked at the adjoining tables. In his opinion, the people seemed intent on their own conversations, not them.

"For just another minute or so. It won't take too long," Bodie groveled.

Juan gave a disgusted huff and pulled up the chair and plopped down onto it. "Say whatever you've got to say then I'm out of here. Forever."

"All right. Just calm down and listen to me a minute." Bodie stared past Juan's head and swallowed visibly before he spoke. "I know my throwing this on you like I did shook you up...but I truly meant everything I said."

"Please."

"I do. I may not have been the best partner a man could have—hell, I wasn't even close—but I've learned from my mistakes. I didn't just hop up and see your face on TV and figure I'd hone in on you again trying to get something out of it for myself. Truth is, I've thought about you every day since you left."

"Save that bullcrap for somebody else."

"Wait. I know it sounds like a bunch of horse dung, but it's the truth. Not a day has gone by that I haven't regretted what a fool I was to let you get away from me."

Juan was apathetic to his words.

"It's not only how you've made yourself into a better man…it's because I realized that you were always too good for me. Since day one." Bodie's eyes misted. "I can remember the first time I laid eyes on you. It was in the Freshman English class. You came in ten minutes late, disrupting the class when you dropped your entire booksack on the floor."

Juan gave a brief smile at the memory. Bodie saw the thaw and pushed his point home.

"I almost had a coronary when I saw that gorgeous bun you had pointed to the sky. Then when you stood up and I saw the rest of you…I almost had to dismiss class. I knew I'd met someone who would change my life forever."

"That's why you chastised me so harshly and told me to stay after class for a conference?" Juan slanted his head, pursed his lips.

"Right. I wanted to see you up close and personal; find out if you might be feeling some of what I was feeling." Bodie reached for Juan's hand again. Juan let him take it without protest.

An ocean of emotions washed over Juan—the rejections he'd encountered from family and friends, the hiding of his lifestyle from the world—before he spoke. "I was. I'd only recently admitted to myself what I was. But I hadn't told my family or friends. Didn't have the courage yet. When we begin talking after class, I felt emotions I'd never felt before. Like a strong tension wire pulling me towards you."

Bodie slowly massaged the palm held in his hands. "I felt the same thing only I knew what it was."

Juan shook his head as if to clear it. "That was a long time ago. I'm not anything like that kid anymore."

"That's not so. Somebody with a good heart like yours never changes."

"Yes we do," Juan answered matter-of-factly. Then he narrowed his eyes and pulled his hand away. "It's just that we have to get messed over repeatedly before it happens."

Chapter 23

"Bartender, give ussssss 'nother round," the blond haired man slurred.

Even though he'd just finished off a toke in the backroom, the stench of liquor halitosis burned its way up the bartender's nostrils and he drew back. "Seems like you've had too many already. Aren't you boys ready to pack it in yet?" The bartender watched the man as he wiped down the bar. Drunks usually became belligerent when he gave the time-to-cut-you-off speech.

"Don't be like that. He's fine," the brown haired man piped in. "Aren't you fine, buddy?" He looked to the blond man for confirmation.

"Sure am. Watch me wa'k a strrrraight line." The blond man slid from the stool and straightened up. He removed his hand from the bar and took two steps before he stumbled forward. He stopped his fall by catching on the edge of the bar.

The bartender kept wiping the counter. "Like I said, time to take it to the house. Besides, it's getting late."

"Hell, why should I go home and you've got all these niccce folks sitting 'round? Besides, you ain't gonna close no time sooooon..."

Bleary eyes stared at the patrons sitting around the room. In his drink-soaked brain, they'd doubled in number. However, the *way* they were sitting seemed strange. He couldn't quite put things right enough in his hazy mind to figure out what it was though. "Why they sitting like that?"

"Like what?" The bartender stopped wiping the counter and looked at the folks in the room. He saw the older man sitting at one table smiling in the direction of the Latin looking guy who seemed to be staring at the Black woman. The man the woman came in with had his back to him and was watching the fire. The way things looked to him, the old man wanted the young guy but the young guy wanted the woman. The Latin dude must have said something to the woman and the man she was with got pissed. Leaning down, he saw the double-barrel shotgun was resting comfortably on the top shelf. He hoped he wouldn't have to use it...but one never knew.

"Seems funny, don't it?" the brown haired man asked. For some unknown reason, the way everything was set up gave him the creeps. Like there was something there he couldn't see...but they could.

"Yeah. I see what you mean," the bartender answered. He knew that something had happened earlier he should have remembered. Somebody else...but...oh, well. The memory escaped him. *Damn, I'm gonna have to give up my weed. I can't remember a damn thing.*

All three heads watched as the older man began laughing in earnest.

24

Tab's laughter irritated Whitey to no end. He clucked his tongue in his mouth as he watched the jowls shake in glee. He crossed his arms across his chest. "Guess you loaded up the jury with your buddies from the CCC."

"Nope. But don't think I wouldn't have if I needed to."

The Citizen Christian Caucus, better known as the CCC, was a lobbying group Tab had formed nearly two decades ago. They said they were there to be the conscience for Americans, but Whitey thought the only agendas they'd furthered were their own. And they had plenty of them: Tough juvenile laws; no welfare; tax increases for the poor, decreases for the rich; separation of the races…all pimped behind the guise of Christianity. They might as well slap a white sheet over their head 'cause in his mind they were just gentrified Klu Klux Klan.

"That in the by-laws of your illustrious organization?"

"*Everything* is covered in the by-laws. If you'd of joined when I asked, you'd know that."

"Naw. I saw the folks you were sporting 'round and I knew me and them wouldn't set right with each other."

"I'm sorry to hear that. I hand-picked every officer myself. Got the ones most likely to stand for our cause."

"And what cause is that again?" Whitey scratched at his head as if confused.

"Christian American values." Tab placed his right hand over his heart as if reciting 'The Pledge of Allegiance.' "The right to live where you want without fear that riffraff will invade the neighborhood and drive prices down. The right to have only the folks *you* want to associate with around you. The right to shove the poor, downtrodden masses back into their burrows. That's the values we stand for."

"That why you let Chit Gilchrist be your front man?" Whitey wheezed.

Chit Gilchrist was as whitebread as they came. Military academy graduate plus the favored oldest son out of a rich family, it was whispered that he wanted to run for governor the next term. Whitey didn't see how that would wash, though. Hell, Chit hadn't ever been elected anything as simple as dogcatcher so why would folks believe he could run a state?

Tab seemed to think Chit's shit didn't stink. He'd flaunted the stiff buffoon before the constituency like he was the next coming of Christ. Tab promoted him and any agenda the CCC proposed from his radio platform. Though Whitey hated to admit it, through some joke of human nature, Chit was one of the most effective lobbyist he'd ever encountered. One meeting with him and people were falling over themselves to support his viewpoint. Personally, Whitey was sick of him and turned the radio off when he heard the nasally voice coming through the speakers.

"One of the best damned ideas I've ever had," Tab affirmed proudly.

"Some might say so," Whitey answered grudgingly. "He's definitely the right choice to be the voicebox for the CCC. Just…"

After a few seconds of silence, Tab asked, "*What?*"

"Goddammit, Tab, the man's an asshole. Just a butthole with ears spewing all the garbage you and your buddies at the CCC want him to spread around. For all his education, he couldn't lead earthworms to dirt," Whitey grumbled.

Tab hitched his lips in a half-grin. "Hell, we don't need him to be able to think. We need him to be able to sway the others to think like we want them to. And that boy is good at that. He waltzes into those offices in his uniform and spit-shined shoes with authority ringing in his voice and lays out our proposal just like we told him to. When he finishes, they think he's speaking for the president himself."

"Ahuh. That how the Juvenile Crime Bill got passed so fast? I mean, one minute they're debating the topic like a hot potato, the next, it's passed in the House and Senate like greased lightening."

Tab nodded effusively. "That was one time we squeezed those good Republicans like a vise. Hell, after the heat we brought down on some of the top players, they couldn't wait to vote yes. Besides, 'ol President Clanton had his own problems and couldn't stand up against the pressure."

"Shit, boy, them laws are criminal!" Whitey exploded.

"Those punks are criminals!" Tab retorted.

"It wadn't enough to kill off Newjean, was it? You had to go after all the ones you felt were 'bad apples'," Whitey accused.

Tab gave a harsh laugh. "Yep. If they'd just listen to their mommas and daddies like good children, they wouldn't have their butts in the slammer."

"It was the school shootings, wasn't it?"

"Partly, but the truth is, the moral fiber of this country has eroded. Kids can't just play with each other and keep themselves occupied. No. They got to hit old folks in the head for a few dollars and kill their parents when they try to correct them. I say give them all some long years in the pokey and it ought to change their minds."

Whitey rubbed his face slowly. "Tab…you been to some of those juvenile facilities?"

"Nope. Ain't got no need to go." Tab picked at his nails.

"You might want to stroll through one sometimes. It ain't no bed of roses for those younguns. They're being beaten, raped and tortured at some of those places. Why? So the so-called good Christian folks can sleep at night."

"If they'd just kept their noses clean, they could be at home sleeping too."

"But what about rehabilitation? Second chances?"

Tab looked at him peculiarly. "You're joking right? About second chances."

"No, I ain't joking one bit." Whitey's tone was severe. "We give adults second chances so why not kids? Why all of a sudden every time a kid does wrong, he's a 'superpredator' and not just a chap that got side-tracked?"

"You believe this crap you saying?" Tab snapped.

"Damn right I do. We slap these kids in jail, offer no rehabilitation, then let them back out on the streets *knowing* they are ten times worse off than when they got locked up in the first place." Whitey voice rises. "Everybody knows what happens to these youngun's when the lights go down. Everybody knows that we *turn* kids into criminals in jail, but it gets swept under the rug like it's somebody else's problem. The way our country handles things, it ain't justice. It's revenge."

Tab looked affronted. "Whitey, when did you become a left-wing liberal petitioning for kid's rights and stuff?"

"When I realized the danger of wasting humans by slapping them behind barbed wire at the drop of a hat. Those same upstanding Christian folks that were all in favor of the harsh penalties then spend the rest of their time bitching about 'wasting taxpayers dollars' because they've got to foot to bill to keep them there. They got what they wanted, didn't they?"

Tab closed his eyes and shook his head. "Now, Whitey—"

Whitey cut him off. "Yeah, wasting taxpayers dollars. The main thing folks are blind to is it also wastes human lives. Twenty folks crowded in a space the size of an average house with nothing to do. Sad tradeoff any way you turn the ball." He clacked his dentures with finality.

"What do you think we should have suggested? Face it. The slap on the wrist method wasn't working. Kids are getting rougher and rougher."

"Naw. Kids are the same as they've always been."

"That ain't so. They're disrespectful. They just don't take to home-training like they use to and—"

"How'd you know?" Whitey interrupted, his tone nasty.

"What?" Tab asked puzzled.

"I said how do *you* know?" His eyes held the plump face captive.

Tab felt the question was weighted with unspoken meaning and proceeded slowly. "What do you mean?" Tab asked quietly.

"I mean, you're spouting off about how home-training ain't working and how they're rotten from birth. Since you've become an authority on child-rearing and all, my question to you is this: What kids have *you* raised?"

Deva

25

Deva broke eye contact first. She thrust her shoulders up and pulled on the shawl before abruptly standing.

"Where're you going?" Ed looked at her in surprise.

"Home. Where I should have stayed my happy behind. If I had known you were going to spend half the damn night criticizing me, I would have passed on this mini-reunion." She turned from him.

Ed surged upwards and grabbed her forearms in a tight hold. "No! You can't leave!"

Deva struggled to remove the offending hand. "Like hell I can't!" she snarled.

Ed held on. "I'm not finished talking. There's plenty of stuff—"

"Remove your hands from the lady," the deep voice cut in menacingly.

"What?" Ed spun towards the voice—irritation evident by his frowns—and saw Jarrel standing impassive at his back…hands fisted.

"I said, remove…your hands…from the lady," Jarrel repeated quietly. The calm tone was rift with barely contained tension. Ed complied immediately. He held his hands in front of him where Jarrel could easily view them.

"Miss Deva, you okay?" His eyes left Ed's face for only a moment while asking this question.

"Yes…I'm fine," Deva whispered.

But Jarrel didn't think she looked fine at all. He stepped between the two bodies. "You ready to go?"

"Yes—"

"No! You can't leave yet. There are some things I need to talk to you about!" Ed pleaded.

Deva turned flashing eyes towards him. "Like what? All I've heard so far is you trashing me."

Ed knew things had escalated out of control. He may have been harsh, but still, he wasn't finished talking. His voice trembled. "Lenora, I know…and I'm sorry. It's just you've changed so much and…I…I'm sorry," he ended lamely. "I still really need to talk to you a bit longer."

"Give her a call at the hotel," Jarrel said and placed a hand beneath Deva's elbow to escort her out.

Ed trotted in front of them, hands wide, placating. "I know you probably hate me right now, but please don't leave just yet. I need to tell you something. It's about Hank Swazy."

Deva's eyes widened. "Hank? What about Hank?" She stepped closer, eyes now slits, and grabbed Ed's arm this time. "He's not trying to sue me, is he?"

Hank Swazy was the unfortunate victim of one of Deva's practical jokes. A hometown boy, Deva had known he'd been in love with her since forever. Ed used to rib her about it all the time. Back then, she'd just ignored the poor fool. However, the way Ed had heard it, on the spur of the moment, she'd flown home and proposed to the young man. They said Hank broke up with his fiancée, quit his job and hopped on the plane Deva had waiting at the community airport.

Unfortunately for him, it apparently was another media ploy to drum up attention for Deva. After five days, she dropped him like a hot potato and left him stranded…in Hawaii. Hank had to call his folks to wire him some money to get home. Then Deva had had the marriage annulled in Mexico.

"Sue you? No, Hank's not about to sue anyone," Ed stated calmly.

"Well, what the hell did you bring up his name for?" Deva was indignant. "If there is ever another person on this earth I never hope to see again, it's Hank."

"You won't."

The way Ed said it made Deva's body chill. She looked at his granite face and realized whatever had happened was serious. She was afraid but still, she ventured the question. "What happened to Hank, Ed?"

Ed's expression never changed as he replied, "I'm surprised you didn't hear, Lenora. He committed suicide yesterday."

The wail leapt from her throat. Deva heard Jarrel calling her name but all she could focus on was Hank's face swimming before her eyes as the entire world turned black.

26

"Yeah, messed over and over again but eventually we get it," Juan asserted.

"Dude, I told you it wasn't like that. When are you gonna believe me?" Bodie insisted.

"When dinosaurs roam the earth again. You've got some damn nerve trying to butter me up and—"

"Well, I guess this means no." Bodie interrupted the tirade by snapping the box closed and placing it in his pocket.

"Damn right, it does." Juan lifted out of his chair again. "Look, if you're through, I'm gonna head on home."

Bodie gave a long-suffering sigh. "I'm not through, but you leave if you want to."

"Good, because I want to."

"Well before you go, have you talked to Dirk Potter lately?"

Dirk was their roommate before Juan left Bodie. He'd not spoken to Dirk since the day he left.

"Nope. Haven't seen or heard from him in years."

"He's probably going to contact you."

"Why? He and I have no history besides being roommates."

Bodie nodded slowly. "He's in trouble. I mean trouble with a capital T."

Juan sat down. Trouble could mean a lot of things—disease, money, police. For gay people you needed to multiply whatever it was by ten. "Trouble. What kind of trouble?" he asked concerned. True, he and Dirk were never close, but he had been a friend.

"Legal."

"So what did he do and why does he want me? I'm not a lawyer."

"He did nothing." Bodie sipped from his beer.

"He's got legal troubles because he did nothing? Come on, man, give me something else to go on."

"Trumped up bullshit, that's what it is." Bodie thumped the can on the table. "He was arrested for having sex with his partner. In my opinion, it's just hogwash."

"What the hell?" Juan was truly confused.

"You heard me right. Dirk was arrested and charged with sodomy because he was having anal sex with a man. His partner."

"Please. Nobody goes to jail for anal sex unless it's forced." Juan knew this was some delay tactic of Bodie's to manipulate him.

"He and his partner did. In fact, he told me they are asking for jail time."

Bodie's impassive face told Juan he wasn't joking. Juan sat up straight. "Wait…this is ridiculous...let me get this straight. Dirk and his partner were having sex and then…" he waved for Bodie to continue.

"The police burst in and arrested them for sodomy."

Juan shook his head. "I don't understand. Is his partner underage or something?"

"No. The man's in his fifties."

"Were the police looking for something else…drugs or stolen goods and they just happened to break in while they were in the act?" Juan offered, trying to wrap his brain around this unbelievable situation.

"No. The police were given a tip and some gay hater on the force decided it was worth the taxpayers dollars to arrest them."

"Who the hell gave the tip?"

"The next door neighbor. Apparently, she was disgusted at the going ons at the house and wanted to put a stop to it."

"When the hell do you call the police because two men are having sex? Were they outside?"

"Nope. In the bedroom with the windows closed and in Texas, sodomy is still on the books as a crime."

Those damn archaic laws. Though society's views had change, many ridiculous laws against sodomy, miscegenation and other lifestyle choices were still on the books.

"Sounds like the 'neighbor' should be arrested as a Peeping Tom."

"She wasn't, though. Dirk and his partner had to post bond and everything. They put up the house as collateral."

"Damn."

"You can say that again. The government wants to police who you have sex with now…even if they are of consenting age and it's not rape."

"Well, we can't let them get away with it. There is no way that any sensible court would entertain a charge of sodomy between consenting, of age adults in this day and time. Hell, one of the freedoms of living in this country is privacy. "

"Dude, you know privacy has gone down the tubes. Big Brother is listening and watching everything we do now. When you log on the internet, 'cookies' keep track of every site you visit. If you hit the right webpage, the government can put a…I don't know what they call it but it's like a tap…and see where you go. Hell, they can even read your emails. Add that to the reality they'll break in and bug your house and workspace if they think they have any little reason to deem it necessary. For all the statements of privacy, we don't really have any."

Juan was stunned. He'd thought those type of tactics were more KGB instead of USA. "Shit."

"Yeah. Then you've got the hackers that love to find out whatever information they want just for the fun of it."

"I know about them," Juan said, remembering his website ordeal. "They can mess up a person pretty bad."

"They can. Some of the ones they caught were only in the *fifth* grade. Fifth grade and hacking. Can you believe it?"

Juan thought about how smart Loam was compared to himself at that age and agreed. "Yeah, I can." He cleared his throat. "What can I do?"

"What you do best. Write about it."

27

"What do…do you mean?" Tab stuttered.

"Last time I checked, when you ate, your family was fed, so again, what kids have *you* raised?" Whitey's eyes burned with fervor.

"Well…I…" Tab stuttered.

"None," Whitey interrupted harshly. "Not a damn one, but all of a sudden you're a damn child psychologist," he spat.

Tab shuffled responses to this assault around in his head. Before he could pull one out of his mouth, Whitey said, "For that matter, where the hell is your wife?" The redness crept up Tab neck. "Why hadn't you gotten hitched after all these years? You ain't in the closet are you, boy?"

This outraged Tab. "Why you wizen up old fart! I can't believe you said some mess like that to *me* of all people!" No, he wasn't married but it wasn't because he didn't want to. Hell, he hadn't met a woman who'd met all his qualifications—meek, humble and believed in him and all his values. Yes, Margie, a dishwater blond he'd dated in the 70's had come close, but she'd spouted off about Nixon and Watergate and that had shut her out of his life forever.

And no way was he having children and no wife. Who in the world wanted a passel of kids strolled all over the place and they had no say in anything? Not him.

"Well I did and you didn't answer the question."

"The question doesn't deserve a damn answer!" Tab barked.

"I think it does. Shit, you damn near seventy and ain't had a wife the one nor a chap with your last name I ever heard about. I've been wondering for years what's wrong with you. Shit, any red-blooded man wants to at least *try* to get a son to carry on his last name. Somebody he can mold into his spitting image. But not you. You don't have didley squat after nearly five decades of chasing tail…or," Whitey cocked his head, "do you have one somewhere you ain't shown the light of day yet?"

"Screw you, old man! I don't have to defend the way I've lived my life to you or anybody else!"

"You got opinions on how others live theirs, so why not?" Whitey pushed.

"That's different. It's what I do. It's—"

"Pshaw!" Whitey cut him off. "You lying to yourself, boy! You just a hypocrite."

"What the hell are you talking about?"

"What the hell do you think? You and your 'do as I say, not as I do' lifestyle!"

"Whitey, I don't know what the hell you're talking about," Tab answered, truly confused.

"Like hell you don't!" Spittle flew from Whitey's mouth. "You've appointed yourself judge and jury over how folks live their lives. Pointing the finger at everyone but yourself."

Tab had faced criticism before but never from someone he'd so cared for. He cleared his throat before he spoke. "Elaborate, please."

Whitey held out his cup for another shot. Tab stared at the bottle but didn't make a move to fill the cup. Whitey finally pulled the bottle to him, tilted it and dribbled a steady stream until it was filled to the brim. His eyes never left Tab's as he drank his fill.

Setting the cup back on the table, Whitey sighed. "Boy, you've lived a charmed life. Oh, I know the beginning might not have been a bed of roses, but once you got your feet on the blacktop, you've been stuck in the fast lane. From the lynching story to now, your life's been smooth sailing. Along the way, though, *you* changed. You went from doing and saying things because you believed in them, to using your power for your personal gain."

"But—" Tab sputtered.

"Hold up. Now you know it's true. You're pushing your personal agendas to million of folks because you can. Ain't lived none of what the average joker does everyday, but you spout off at the mouth about what they *should* do and how they *should* live and it's wrong. It's just plain wrong."

"That's your opinion. You don't have to do everything in life to know what a person *should* do." Tab narrowed his eyes. "Besides, don't forget that whatever I learned in this business, right or wrong, I learned it at your knee. You showed me all the tricks of the trade."

"I showed you *some* tricks. I hadn't never gone to the level you've gone to."

"And what level is that?"

"As low as a snake's belly."

"That's a lie!"

"Of course you'd see it that a way. But the truth is, you spend so much time in other folk's business, yours is in shambles. Like I said, no wife, no kids—"

"My business is just fine. Why I'm one of the richest men in the country," Tab nearly shouted. He was affronted by this attack on his lifestyle.

"Boy, you can lie to a lot of folks, but just remember, somewhere, somebody knows the truth. And the truth is…" Whitey's finger nearly touched between Tab's eyes. "you are a damn mess."

"Whitey—" Tab began, a warning tingeing his voice.

"Be honest, boy! You can't face yourself in the mirror, not the 'real' you anyway. That's why you singled out Tondal Keyes like you did."

Keyes was a black rookie who the media touted as one of the greatest quarterbacks in history and the main reason why his team, the Baton Rouge Wildcats, were in the playoffs marching steadily towards the SuperBowl. Tab had voiced his lone opinion and called the man a 'watermelon eating ape who threw like a girl.' The media response had been critical. In fact, the higher ups at the station had called him on the carpet about it.

Tab took it all in stride. Hell, if they talked too much, he'd just take his show to another station. They backed down and shut up.

Flash anger rose in Tab. "I singled out that chump because they were making too much of a show about an average black guy that happened to be in the right place, at the right time."

"That's how luck and opportunity work, boy! Half the folks that make it big aren't better than the next man. They just happened to be ready when the chance came!" Whitey boomed. "Shit, a kid out of the projects that turns into one of the NFL's greatest quarterbacks? You ought to be drinking that news up like it's champagne."

"I hate champagne. Anyway, the man ain't as good as a Joe Montana, Steve Young or Joe Namath on a bad day. Hell, ain't nobody ever gonna be better than Joe Namath."

"Yeah, that's why plenty of folks have passed his records already," Whitey smirked. "You know, my *sources* say that it was just a tactic since you're under pressure trying to divert attention from your little Valium addiction. In fact, even though you've managed to keep everything hush-hush, they plan to break the story wide open."

A sheen of perspiration appeared on Tab's face. He didn't realize anyone knew about the Valium. "Go on," he said.

"Is it true?"

Tab looked at the ceiling and patted his chest searching for a cigar. Finding one, he bit off the tip and placed it between his teeth. He sat elbows on the table and leaned forward, eyes darting around the room, searching for any eavesdroppers.

Not seeing any, he answered, "Whitey, I do use some prescription drugs…but it's for a back injury I got a couple of years ago. The police contacted me a few weeks ago. Seems that some pharmacy got my prescription mixed up and when they contacted the office, they had some new help and they said they didn't see the prescription in the chart. It was legit, though. There was just a mix-up. That's all." Tab's eyes pleaded for Whitey to believe him.

"A mix-up."

"Yep. A simple mix-up. I'm sure it will all pass over."

Whitey folded him arms. "Tab, boy, that probably won't happen."

Tab sat up. "Why do you say that?"

Whitey showed his dentures in a grotesque caricature of happiness. "According to my *sources*, they plan to pick you at the station and charge you in the morning."

"Shit."

Deva

28

Jarrel's face swam back into focus. Deva stared between him and Ed, hoping beyond hope that what she'd heard was a lie. Their faces told the story, though. It was true. Hank was dead. Suicide.

The press was gonna have a field day with this. This thought panicked her and she tried to lift herself from the floor.

"Hold still, Ms. Deva," Jarrel said, a hand restraining her.

"No! I've got to get out of here!" Deva pushed at his hand, trying to rise.

"Hold on, Lenora. Rest for a minute," Ed said soothingly.

Deva stared at his face. "My God, Ed, it's really true, isn't it? Hank's dead," she cried.

"I'm afraid so."

This answer brought on a fresh stream of tears. "I didn't mean for things to go like this," she blubbered.

"We never do. But when you play with other folk's feelings and lives, there is no telling the outcome." Ed sounded harsh and Deva felt the rebuke to her core.

"Could you just ease up on her for a minute?" Jarrel snarled at Ed.

Ed stayed silent.

Deva thought about the press again. "Ohmigod! Ohmigod! People will say that I caused him to kill himself!"

"Shhhhh. Calm down, Ms. Deva. Folks won't think that just because you were once married to the guy, you caused his suicide. He might have had some other problems. We don't know."

"I don't understand why my mother or somebody never called and told me a thing. They had to have known."

"Well, it just happened so maybe she didn't want you to worry," Ed supplied.

"What was she waiting on? For the press to spring it on me?" Deva gave Ed an incredulous stare. "This was something that my mother knew I'd need to know. I just don't understand why she didn't tell me." The tears slid unchecked down her face, tears for poor Hank, for life misjudgments…for herself. Deva had to know. "Ed, what happened?"

"Well, they said he'd been depressed since the wedding fiasco. You seemed to have taken him to heaven and back." Ed gave a little smile. "Anyway, you know he'd already broken off with his fiancée and quit his job—and jobs are hard to come by down our way—and neither one wanted any parts of him when he returned. It seems that he'd said some ugly things to both his employer and fiancée before he boarded your jet. Burned all his bridges, you might say. Then he started drinking…had a few run-ins with the law—you know that was totally unlike his scared tail—and continued on this downhill spiral until his mother returned home two days ago and found him swinging in the bathroom."

Deva wailed again at this news. The fact that he killed himself was one thing but to *hang* himself to death was unbearable. Why couldn't he have taken some pills or something? Anything but hang himself.

"Did you have to tell her all the details?" she heard Jarrel say to Ed.

"She asked, didn't she?" Ed replied.

"But can't you see that she's in no state to hear this mess?"

"It's a mess she created, my brother," Ed retorted.

It was true and Deva knew it like she knew her own name. She'd caused a man to kill himself. She'd used him carelessly; a joke simply because he was convenient and knew he was still in love with her. She might not have planned for things to go like they had, but they had. God help her. "The press will crucify me. Shit, my album sales will plummet!" Deva covered her face.

"Hank's dead and you're worried about your image and your album sales?" Ed sat back, his face a mask of distaste.

"It's not like that—"

"Like what? A man killed himself—probably because of you—and one of the first things out of your mouth is 'My album sales will plummet!'" Ed reminded her none too gently. "But don't worry, Lenora. Hank was just a nobody to you and the rest of the world." Ed's eyes blazed. "His passing will get a mention in the local paper and life will move on. Even if some reporter does mention his death, people will probably think he wasn't good enough for your Royal Highness butt anyway!"

Ed's words made her anger surface. "That's enough! You jump on your high horse because Hank killed himself…but I didn't do it. He did it. He *chose* to hang himself. What about? Who the hell knows? Maybe me, maybe not. So don't start blaming me for his weak ass mind. Hank wasn't like we remember. He'd turned snotty."

"Really," Ed drawled. "Please elaborate."

Deva hadn't told anyone outside of her staff what had really happened but it looked like the world would be asking her so she might as well start. "Me marrying Hank was a publicity stunt."

"I knew it and—"

"Hear me out. Please." Deva wiped a stray tear from her lower lid. "Hank was a willing partner. We'd agreed to give things a shot and if we parted ways before six months was up, I'd give him fifty thousand dollars cash." She ignored Ed's surprised face and continued. "Well, seems like Hank had big plans for himself. He acted like he'd hit the Lotto—clothes, jewelry, furs for *himself*. This was by day three. Then he started the Mr. Prima Dona routine."

"What's that?" Ed snapped.

"He'd lay around all day and expect my people to jump at his every whim while he whined constantly—the towels needed to be fluffier, the suites larger, the champagne more expensive…nothing was good enough for him." Deva shook her head. "When my staff started complaining that he was trying to change my schedule around, I decided to speak to him. What a joke of a conversation! I'm talking calmly and he goes slap off! Turns chairs over, tosses the lamp into the wall—and he wasn't paying for shit! Just mooching off of me. I knew then that this idea wasn't going to work out. There was no way in hell I was putting me and my staff though his tantrums any longer. I wrote him a check for the fifty grand and left on my jet."

"But Hank didn't have any money. They say he had to have some wired to him."

"Well I gave him what I owed him. Hell, he probably spent it at the casino trying to act like a High Roller. We had to settle up nearly twenty thousand in markers he'd taken out at the PALACINO." Deva's nostrils flared at the memory. She worked hard for her money and didn't believe in wasting it on things she couldn't see. Her voice got ice cold. "Hank made out like a bandit in my opinion. So if he killed himself, it had nothing to do with me. It was his choice."

Ed's hands trembled as he slowly reached to touch Deva. He knew he'd been way too harsh on her. Rubbing her arms lightly, he spoke just above a whisper. "I'm sorry. I didn't know."

"Nobody did. I just thought he'd take the money home and live out a good life. Guess he wasn't ready to go back to being a regular Joe, huh?" Deva smiled slightly.

"It's hard to go back low once you get a taste of being high," Ed commented quietly.

Thinking of her zenith ride from her lowly beginnings to the height of popularity…there was no way Deva could dispute the raw truth.

Sydney Molare'

Sydney Molare'

Juan Rodriguez

29

"Hmmm. Write about it." Juan stroked his chin as book ideas floated around his head.

"Yeah, something spectacular. Deep. You know some shit to expose and shame the ones still acting like anal sex is a sin."

"Well it *is* still on the books in a lot of places," Juan joked.

"Doesn't mean the shit is right, though." Bodie turned and took a gulp of his beer.

"True. It definitely doesn't mean that." Juan scratched his head. "You know, most of my writing to date has dealt with my situations and feelings. I've never focused on anything outside of what was going on in my world. Maybe this would be the type of project I need to 'step outside my comfort zone.'" Juan gave Bodie a questioning eye.

"However you want to term it, just write that sucker!" Bodie chuckled.

"Hard to believe that in this new millennium we still have to deal with this antiquated shit."

"That's because the archaic assholes running the show still believe in that antiquated shit."

Juan snapped his fingers. "I've got it! What if I wrote about a straight couple in a gay world. Flip the script. Somebody blows the whistle on them when they see them having sex in the infamous missionary position. The cops barge in and they are hauled to jail just for having sex. Think they would see the irony of the situation then?" Juan asked.

"Probably not. Narrow assed folks can't see past their blinders. They'll most likely ban that sucker before it hits the shelf. "

"You think so?"

"Yep. 'Cause if they don't, then they'll have to come up with some *real* sensible answers for Little Johnny and Joanne and they can't," Bodie finished.

"The more I think about it, the more I like this idea. Shit, I'll donate the proceeds to the Dirk Potter Legal Fund or something like that. Yeah, I'm feeling this one," Juan nodded, his adrenaline pumping as the story line jumped around his head.

"That's what I'm talking about!" Bodie shouted, then lifted his glass towards Juan again. "Cheers?"

"For real." Juan clinked his can with Bodie's glass.

Chapter 30

Suddenly, thunder boomed then a bolt of lightning seemed to flash inside the room. A vision-numbing light filled the space and all eyes squinted in pain while cries of "What the hell?" "My God, what's happening?" "Shit!" rang out.

As sight slowly returned to normal, hands kept rubbing eyes as though they didn't believe what they were witnessing. Before them stood a man surrounded by a pulsing white glow. The average person would described him as a good looking African American man wearing a sparkling white suit—fingers superstar beringed—surrounded by a halo of light that seemed to be…a living, breathing entity in its own right.

Tab recovered first. "What the hell is this? This some kind of joke?" He looked around expectantly. The Black chick and Hispanic guy were glued to their seats, eyes wide, mouths open. He knew then something was terribly wrong but pushed it away; looked for a logical explanation for everything. "Whitey, what—?" He stopped as he realized that Whitey was no where to be found. With an abrupt start, he saw neither the guy the girl had been speaking with nor the man the Puerto Rican had been talking to.

Looking around the room in bewilderment, Tab realized that except for him, the woman, the Puerto Rican and the new black guy, the others in the bar seemed…frozen. The blond guy was parallel to the floor, suspended in a free-fall, while his partner had a glass halfway to his mouth. The bartender's back was bent as though he had been looking for something beneath the bar when he was…stilled. The black guy the girl came in with was crouched, a scowl seared into his visage.

This confirmed it for Tab: Supernatural. He felt the blood pumping in his ears, swishing through his brain at freeway speed. A shiver ran up his spine as he turned back to the stranger who stood there, a smile of shared conspiracy on his red lips. He winked. Tab dropped into his chair as if slapped.

Deva seemed to come out of her trance. "Who are you?" she asked quietly, her voice surprising herself. Her survey of the room mirrored Tab's so in her mind, she knew should be shrieking and screaming, not asking questions in a normal tone. But no matter the answer, she was positive that whatever this person in front of her was, it was not of this world.

The stranger began clapping his hands, his smile stretching from cheek to cheek. "Bravo! Congratulations! You guys were just as magnificent as I knew you would be!" he exclaimed, still clapping.

Juan snapped forward in his chair. "What are you talking about? Who are you? What is this about?" The hand clenching the rosary felt on fire.

The clapping stopped as abruptly as it began. You could hear a mice fart…that is if mice fart. The stranger looked puzzled then smiled as if this whole setup was an inside joke they had pre-planned. "You know who I am. I'm your master! The one you serve!" he exclaimed, like his explanation was quite reasonable.

"Master? Buddy, I don't know who you think you are, but I don't have a master," Tab stated in a strong but raspy voice.

"Of course you do. We all do." The man paused as if to let his words settle themselves in their minds. Then his voice reverberated around the room, his lips never moving, "I AM YOUR MASTER! THE ONE YOU WILLINGLY SERVE!"

Deva yelped before slapping her hands over her ears. Juan toppled his chair backwards. Tab clutched at his chest. The stranger seemed to swell and grow; the light's intensity increasing exponentially.

Deva screamed, "Who are you! What do you want from us!" Her eyes skittered from face to face, a harried search for some…normalcy.

The stranger shook his head sorrowfully. "They denied Jesus so why wouldn't you deny me?" He shrugged his shoulders as to say 'I should have known better.' "Well, I'm called by many names—Prince of Darkness, Father of All Lies, The Deceiver, demon, archfiend, beast, Beelzebub—one of my personal favorites—dybbuk, enfant terrible, Evil one, fiend, hellion, Antichrist, Mephistopheles, sin Abaddon, Apollyon, Belial—and of the course the usual, Devil, Satan and Lucifer. So many choices! Now, you may call me Master, or if you want to be informal about it, Luke will do," he finished with another dazzling smile.

Tab was the first to respond. "Please stop this…this…joke. Where are our friends?" He looked around the room again.

"Yes, where are they? One minute I'm talking with Ed, the next, you're here and he's…gone." Deva looked around the room again.

"They are gone. Pfffst!" Luke waved his hands in the air.

"We see that they are gone. But where?" Juan prodded. His mind refused to accept that there was actually a reality where people vanished in thin air.

"They are gone," Luke stated with finality.

"Just gone. 'Pfffst,' as you said," Juan responded. "Are you a magician or something?"

"No, no magician. I am what I am. Your *master*."

Tab threw his hands into the air.

"You see, your *friends* are already inhabitants of my resort—Hades. I just summoned them back to assist me."

"You mean they're d…dead?" Juan stuttered, confused and now scared again.

"D-E-A-D. Dead to you…not to me." Luke winked.

"They can't be dead," Deva asserted, hysteria bubbling on the outer fringes of her sanity. "Dead people don't hold conversations!"

"Oh, but my dear, they are dead as dead can be. Let me see if I can explain this better." Luke rubbed his goatee. "Juan, your friend Bodie's…ah… *habits* finally caught up to him. He passed into my kingdom six months ago from liver failure, kidney failure and AIDS. Must have been something he ate or *sucked*." Luke giggled before looking at Deva.

"Deva, Ed…how can I say this nicely?" Luke thought a moment before he continued with a shrug of his shoulders. "Ed couldn't cut the mustard. Punked out. Slit his wrist like a girl two days ago. They won't find him until his rotting body begins to stink up his hallway in about…three more days."

"No!" Deva screamed, hand clamping over her mouth.

"Yes!" Luke mimicked her actions and giggled again. His eyes left Deva and focused on Tab. "Now Tab, ole Whitey is still breathing—artificially—but he *is* still breathing. Anyway, he's down at Charity Hospital on life support. The doctors know he's brain dead but his wife won't let them pull the plug on him. The breathing dead. Uhmp. What can I say? Denial *is* a disease." Luke gave a full belly laugh this time.

"Let me tell you, he damn near burst the gate open when he came through!" Luke gave them an incredulous look. "I mean, the gargoyles could barely roll out the Fire Red Carpet before he trotted around the corner. Uncouth as hell!" Luke snorted.

One lone tear trailed down Tab's face unchecked.

"Are you *crying*? Tab McGrifth…crying?" Deva's head swiveled to look at Tab. "See, even she knows that doesn't go together in a sentence. Anyway, save your tears. You'll see all your old buddies soon." Luke winked at him.

"Tab McGrifth? *You're* Tab McGrifth?" Deva asked tentatively, eyes boring into Tab's.

"That's right." Tab wiped the tears from his eyes and squinted at Deva. "Have been from day one and will always be!"

"W…what?" Juan stuttered, surprise evident in his voice.

"You asshole!" Deva screeched. "You damn near destroyed my career!"

"Woman, who the hell are you?" Tab spat.

Deva sat straighter in the chair. "You've heard of Deva?"

Tab's lips curled in a sneer. "You're Deva?" He looked her up and down as she nodded. "Guess the photos are air-brushed." He then looked over at Juan. "Since we're all famous here, who are you?"

"Juan Rodriguez, author."

Tab's eyebrow quirked as comprehension dawned. "The fag writer?"

The blood bubbled in Juan's head but he pushed the red haze down and replied, "I am an author of alternative literature."

"So that's a yes, you are the fag author?" Tab smiled as he repeated the slur.

"Lifestyle choices don't make me a fag!" Juan yelled.

"Nope, poking up butts makes you a fag," Tab corrected him.

Deva stood. "You jerk! Who the hell told you you had the right to tear somebody's life apart?"

Tab leaned back and crossed his arms. "Well, little lady, you put your life—especially your body—out there. All I do is make comments about what I see. It's not like I'm the paparazzi following you around. I see what America sees on billboards, in magazines and on television."

Juan seethed. "But you think you have license to put your own torqued 'spin' on it and what's so bad is people believe that crap you spew."

"Like I said, I comment on what I see and hear. Nothing more, nothing less."

"Bullshit. You made me sound like I'm one step from a streetwalker." Deva shook with flash rage before taking a step closer to Tab's chair, her hand curled into a fist.

Luke cleared his throat loudly, gaining their attention again. "Okay folks, we've all met and gotten acquainted. My next question is simple: Are you ready to enter the Kingdom?"

Tab looked away. Deva sat back into her seat, her hand rubbing together constantly. Juan fingered the beads vigorously, mouthing a silent prayer.

"Stop it!" Luke screamed at him. "If that's the path you wanted to take, you had plenty of time to do so before now. You are through with *Him.* If you pray to anybody, pray to *me.*" Luke's index finger stabbed his chest.

Juan continued rubbing the rosary. He recalled some of the lessons he'd learned from childhood and felt emboldened. "I don't know what you are but you are *not* the Devil. You don't look anything like him."

Luke sighed. "People are always saying that. I guess you only imagine me like this." Luke's face bubbled then melted and morphed. First the eyes became slit orbs then the skin scaled. The hands and feet elongated into sharp claws while twin, bulbous protrusions forced themselves from his forehead. A forked tongue snaked out of his mouth and flitted in the air. The pungent smell of sulfur suffused the room. "Better?"

No one dared breathed.

"Kind of takes your breath away, doesn't it?" he asked with a giggle. "Let me change back because I need your full attention tonight." Within seconds, he'd resumed his previous human form. Without waiting for a response from anyone, he pulled a chair out, turned it around and seated himself, arms draped across the rail. "I can tell from your expressions you don't understand what's happening." No one moved.

"I empathize with your confusion but please don't be confused. My job here is to welcome you into the Kingdom." Luke opened his arms wide.

"*Dios*!" Juan exclaimed.

Luke's eyes narrowed; the irises reddened. "I would appreciate if you would refrain from mentioning *His* name. It pisses me off. And believe me, you do *not* want to piss me off!"

No muscle twitched, no breath was expelled as they watched Luke.

Luke's facial features shifted again—slant to the eyes, dark straight hair, round face. Asian. "Let me ask you all something. You understand the concept of Free Will, right?"

Three heads nodded in concert.

"Good. You understand the concept of *Him* and me." Luke didn't wait for an answer. "Now it's very simple. You asked me to give you your heart's desire…and I have. So I'm thinking since I've held up to my end of the bargain, it's time for you to give me what I want. And believe me when I tell you, paying me back will be a mother." Luke cackled in glee and clapped his hands some more.

The only other sound heard was three hearts galloping in sync.

Chapter

31

"You guys sure look tense," Luke said as his eyes scanned each of them. "Let's lighten things up a bit." With that, Luke crossed his eyes while his face melted and morphed once again. His complexion became pinker, hair sprouted around his mouth and his hair grew inches. When the transformation was completed, he strongly resembled Tom Cruise.

"What do you think?"

"Stop it. Stop this cruel joke right now!" Juan spoke stridently.

"What joke? This is for real," Luke asserted. "I *am* Lucifer, those people are in suspended animation," he motioned to the frozen people, "and you guys owe me your souls. Now where is the joke in any of this?" He held his palms upwards.

"Wait," Deva spoke up, "I may not have visited a church in a minute, but I don't ever recall praying for your help."

"What about 'I didn't care if he was Old Satan himself, I was gonna give everything I had to see if he could make my dreams come true?' Forgot that, huh? Well I didn't."

"B…but I was just joking, just saying some old…cliché. I didn't mean it!" Deva wailed, surging from her chair. There was no way in the world anyone could believe that she'd actually *want* to be in cahoots with the Devil! It was unimaginable.

"You mean to say that at the very moment you uttered that sentence you didn't want what was offered to you with everything you had?" Luke inquired, eyebrow raised.

"No!"

"De-va…" Luke questioned.

"I mean yes, I said it but I didn't mean it like you are insinuating. I would never forge a pact with the devil to make my dreams come true! I just wanted the opportunity. The pure opportunity!" Deva cried out.

"So why didn't you say, 'Thank you, Jesus!' or something along those lines if that was so? Why be so willing to possibly dance with the devil to get what you wanted if you didn't plan to pay *all* the price? Why say something that most people would never utter when a blessing is bestowed on them?" Luke countered.

Deva stared blankly. The question had her stumped. Why didn't she? Was she really so superficial that she'd been willing to forego everything she'd learned in church for a piece of heaven on earth? At any price? "I…I don't know," she finally whispered then slumped back into her seat.

Tab cleared his throat. "Now let me get this straight. You're saying that just because we *might* have said some…things in the heat of the moment, it's a binding contract? Uh uh. I ain't buying that. Ain't no way that the Lord lets things work like that."

Thunder boomed and the building began to shake violently. The walls buckled inward as though they were ready to implode. The chandelier swung dangerously and plaster dust rained around them.

"My God, is it an earthquake?" Deva screamed as she stood and looked around the shaking building.

Just as quickly as it began, it ended.

"Nope. Just me. I told you all not to use *His* name in any form *because* it pisses me off! No Lord, Jesus, God, Dios or any other pet name you have for *Him!* Understood?" Smoke streamed from Luke's flared nostrils.

"Calm down. We understand," Juan placated.

"I don't think you do. Seems to me that if you all were so far on *His* side, you'd have visited the inside of one of His shrines lately. When was the last time any of you set foot in a church?" Luke questioned.

Deva knew the last time she'd gone to church was when she lived at home and that was more than five years ago. The thought of going into a church—unless it was a funeral or wedding—hadn't crossed Tab's mind in decades. Juan, a former acolyte, hadn't been to Mass in nearly three years. Once the success came, he just didn't have time to go. Sunday mornings had become catch-up-on-sleep time.

"Exactly," Luke stated, reading their minds. "Now you are sitting here trying to 'get saved' just because I've come to claim what you owe me? Talk about hypocrites!"

Luke ran a hand across his face and sighed. "Look, it's really quite simple. I play by the rules *He* set up. *He* sent down the Ten Commandments and that's supposed to be your guidebook. Now the one flaw in *His* whole plan is what I mentioned earlier—Free Will. Yessiree, that beautiful bit of leniency on *His* part leveled the playing field.

"See, I've never forced anyone to do anything. I just put the myriad of temptations out there and *you*, not me, decided whether or not you wanted to take them. But when you took it, like everything else in life, you've got to pay for it. Ain't nothing free. And depending on how fast and often you take the temptations determines how quickly you get to see me." Luke waggled his eyebrows then grinned, showing superstar white teeth.

"You guys need to be thanking me! I normally don't pay a personal visit to escort people into the Kingdom. Usually, I just have the gargoyles role out the Fire Red Carpet and let your skinny/fat/rich/poor behinds scamper in on your own. But I took time out of my busy schedule—do you know how time consuming it is to run Hades?—to pay a *personal* visit. I had to. You guys have increased my kingdom tenfold. Just by your actions, you've sent millions of people my way."

Juan surged out of his chair. "Bullshit! That's pure bullshit! You might *think* you are the devil or whatever, but I've never done anything to encourage people to follow you!" he spat.

"*Au contraire*, my dear devotee. Since you published your missive, millions of men have 'gotten in touch with their feminine side.' They've come out of the closet in droves. Left wives, children and changed lifestyles to live how they believe they truly are. At some point, these newly 'released' souls decided they needed to voice their rights so they organized and got them! 'Committed' couples get benefits, support, etc. Now marriage, one of *your* most vocal platforms…do you see where I'm going with this?" Sarcasm drips from Luke's voice.

"Not particularly. The intention of my novel was to write about *my* exper—"

"Doesn't matter what your intent was. The end result was a manual for coming out," Luke interrupted. " 'The Alternative Lifestyle Bible' I believe they are calling it? Are you really blind to the effect your book had on the world?" Luke shook his head. "Let me ask you something. What do you think is the reason for the rise in homosexuality? Before you answer that, I want you to understand I have no problem with your book. I think it was a great product." He gave another superstar white smile.

"I don't know the answer to that but I do know that writing a book didn't 'turn' anyone gay. We were born like this," Juan asserted.

"Oh, now *He* makes mistakes? All those scriptures are wrong…" Luke snapped his fingers. "I know, they were transcribed incorrectly." He snorts. "Works for me but I don't know how *He* feels about that statement. Born to sodomize. Sounds like good old Free Will to me."

"Think what you want, but it's true. You're born either straight or gay," Juan finished.

"That's a load of crap, Bud," Tab interjected. "You're gay 'cause you want to be gay. Ain't no gay or straight chromosomes. It's a choice."

"You don't know what you are talking about!" Juan snarled. "I didn't sit down and say 'Hey, I want to be gay,' I have *always* been gay. I wasn't molested, didn't have a traumatic childhood and our family never watched television. Yet, I have *always* known I preferred men. If it's not something innate, then what is it?" Juan responded.

"Hell, I'm no fairy psychologist—"

"I can't believe you said fairy psychologist!" Juan sputtered

"Kids, kids, let's not squabble," Luke said, boredom evident in his tone.

Tab continued unfazed, "— but like…ah…" he motioned to Luke, "…ah, like the man said, all the scriptures can't be wrong."

Luke turned his syrupy voice towards a now red Juan. "Now Juan, be honest. You never once thought that what you wrote—especially as controversial as it was—*might* have caused harm to someone? Might have caused a negative effect?"

"I've never given it any thought. Maybe if I *knew* that to be true, I would not have written my book. Heck, anybody can read something and cause themselves harm. You can't blame me for somebody else's state of mind," Juan huffed.

"So you say." Luke chuckled lightly.

"What's so funny?" Juan snarled.

"Just wondering what the good folks upstairs just wrote down about that statement."

"I agree with Juan. Just because we are in the limelight all the time doesn't mean that people should do what we do," Deva chimed in.

"Okay. Deva, let me ask you this. Have you ever considered that girls might want to dress like you, wear their hair like you, try stunts like you?"

Yes, millions of fans wore what she wore, mimicked her antics and every mannerism, but so what? She was a star and that's what people do: Imitate stars. "I don't control what people do. When I'm on stage, I'm doing *my* thing. I'm not thinking about what folks might do afterwards. They pay for a show and I give them one!" Deva shouted.

"Little touchy aren't we?" Luke smirked. "So you are saying that at no point did any action you…*performed* influence another person?"

"I'm saying that people seeing me should see the positives I promote."

"Skimpy clothes, nipples exposed, underage lovers…help me out with the positives here," Luke suggested.

"You're focusing on what may be misconstrued as negatives. What about my work with the women's shelter? The money I donated? My 'Voter Up' campaign?" Deva countered. She was sick of folks remembering a little slip up here and there. But nobody wanted to harp on the great things she'd done in life.

Luke bobbed his head. "All admirable, I admit. But in twenty years do you think people will remember that? Or your naked boob at the Superball?"

Deva remained silent.

Luke trained his eyes on Tab. "Any defense you want to give about your life actions? Now is the time."

"My life speaks for itself. I've never done anything I would be ashamed of," Tab responded, chin rising. He forced down the thoughts niggling his brain determined to stand firm on his statement.

"Nothing? Take a minute and think," Luke pushed.

Tab stared at the wall a moment as ugly, undisputable images he'd long ago pushed to the back of his mind bank paraded to the forefront, then looked back at Luke and nodded. "I'll admit there may be a few things that have been…misrepresented in the press, but for the most part, I'm happy with my life."

Luke snorted and rolled his eyes upwards.

Tab saw and bristled. "Look, we're all tired and would really like to go home. Let's get this…show or whatever over with and call it a night," Tab stated, eyes glued on Luke.

"Well if you all are ready to go," Luke began standing up from the chair, "let's go!"

"Wait a minute!" Deva screamed. "*I* don't want to go any place with you especially if you are the devil." She looked at Tab as if he'd lost his mind.

"Hey, I've said what I came to say, you guys are tired and ready to leave, what more do you want? Scared? Don't worry, you won't feel a thing," Luke smiled and winked.

"Luke, listen!" Deva felt her voice rising but was powerless to bring it back to normal tone. These other two might think he wasn't the devil but Deva *felt* even if he wasn't, he definitely was *not* a better alternative. "I can't speak for anyone else, but I know that there is always grace and redemption up until the moment I die. Yeah, I might have participated in some dishonorable things and had some sinful public actions that millions of folks copied, but you can't tell me you can just waltz in here and take my soul because of some words said in jest and there is nothing I can do about it. *He* doesn't work like that!" she spat. Then drawing on her Baptist upbringing, she closed her eyes, outstretched her palms and took the biggest chance of her life. "Our father, which art in heaven, hallowed be thine name—"

Luke kicked the chair into the wall where it exploded.

"—Thy kingdom come. Thy will be done on earth as it is—"

The smoke billowed from Luke's nostril. Juan walked beside Deva and grasped a hand. Together they continued.

"—in Heaven. Give us this day—"

Fire wisped from Luke's hair, his eyes reddened. Tab sprang from his chair and grabbed Deva's other hand. He closed his eyes and focused. The words crawled upwards from the basement of his memory bank and he added his voice.

"—our daily bread and forgive us our sins as we forgive those who sin against us—"

"STOP!" Luke yelled, his voice reverberating around the overheating room.

Deva felt something growing within her. *Faith?* Emboldened, she opened her mouth wider and allowed her voice to segue into her melodious alto, "—and lead us not into temptation and deliver us from e-vil!—"

Luke screamed loud and long. Eardrums popped. The building shook. The ground shifted. The trio pitched forward, holding onto each other's hand, their voices never faltering.

Juan rusty tenor rose high and loud."—for thine is the Kingdom, and the power and the glory forever. Amen."

The air crackled. Hearts thumped loudly. Hair stood on end. As eyes opened, they saw Luke was fully ablaze. The smell was overpowering; the heat intense. Hands squeezed each other tighter as Luke walked within two feet of them. The heat melted Deva's wig, the molten synthetic strands dripping and burning her face. Smoke rose from their clothes. Still, they held on to each other.

"You all have made a *big* ass mistake! I didn't come all this way to give you a second chance! You've all had second, third, five thousand chances and *you* chose to continue in your ways!" The sulfur smell nearly made Deva faint, but she held firm as Luke continued.

"There were no guns, no drugs, no nothing! I never enticed you! *I* am your MASTER! The one you *willingly* chose to serve!" The flames on Luke's head flared nearly to the ceiling. The dry wood crackled and caught fire.

"You know the hardest part? I didn't come to you! You came to me! Now I'm here to collect what you promised me—your souls—and y'all have gotten holier-than-thou on a brother! Let's be honest. In your darkest hour, while you were calling for *Him*, you were thinking of me—the Dark Angel—too! Don't think I don't know it! I'm just like *Him*—omnipotent, omnipresent and all knowing." A flame spewed from Luke's mouth.

"Did you really believe that I would allow you to play me? To allow me to give you everything that your heart desired, simply because you asked me to, and I get *nothing* out of the deal? No soul, just a 'thanks for all the great times but we don't need you anymore?' Well, you have lost your minds! You called, I did as you asked...now *pay* me!" The fire on the ceiling ran to the four corners.

Deva closed her eyes against the smoke drifting down, determined that if she was about to die, the praises of God would be on her lips at the end. "The Lord is my shepherd and I shall not want—"

"Didn't I tell you not to say *His* name!" Luke screamed. He grabbed the interlocked hands. The smell of flesh burning filled their nostrils as the skin bubbled then blackened. The pain was more excruciating than any of them had ever felt before, yet they didn't release each other, didn't scream out in pain. The skin split over the fingers and bone became visible.

"God, you are the way, the truth and the light! Forgive us!" Juan yelled through the pain. *My God, save Zeus and Loam from this!*

"Forgive us, God! Forgive us, God! Forgive us, God! Forgive us, God!" Tab blubbered, pain etching his voice.

Deva and Juan joined him and in triplicate they yelled this over and over again. Deva yelled because she knew there was greater strength in numbers. Juan yelled because he knew that with an earnest heart, God was listening and he'd never been more earnest than he was at this particular moment. Tab yelled because he was more scared than he'd ever been in his entire life. He'd never been a church goer and his entire repertoire of Bible verses was exhausted so he yelled the first thing that came to mind. He had no idea of what else to do.

Suddenly, Luke released their hands.

Chapter 32

Their voices died down after a few minutes. They opened their eyes to see the ceiling was no longer burning and Luke had returned to his human form, white suit unmarred, face unreadable. Then he spoke.

"I see I have misjudged you three after all." Not one muscle flinched. "All the fame, the accolades and you repay me like *this*." Disgust was evident on his face. "In that case, I will give you one more opportunity to see who you truly serve." He looked at each of them. "Some of you know the parable about the rich man getting to heaven?" Juan nodded in affirmation. "How about the man who wastes his talents?" Deva nodded this time. "Good. Since we've gone back to being 'right' let's go all the way back to right from the start. Here's the deal: This is your last opportunity to decide whose side you truly want to play on. And while you are deciding, you will lose the tremendous talent I have blessed each of you with and which made you money." They all gasped.

Luke was amused. "Harsh? I'm thinking not harsh enough after this fiasco you all pulled on me." The smile left his face. "*Him* this, *Him* that, singing his praises like you and *He* are on first name basis.

'We love you, we thank you, help us!'" Luke quoted then dropped his hands. "Why didn't you call on *Him* and pray about the situation when you were offered the deal of a lifetime?"

No one offered a suggestion.

"The answer is simple: Because *He* wasn't even a thought when you received your bounty!" Luke thundered.

No one disputed him.

"I see I've taken your smart-alecky mouths away. I tell you what. I'll help you out, let you see what's in store for you. Then you might want to reconsider whose side you really want to play on the rest of your life," Luke said, a large grin springing back to his face.

The smile left Luke's face and he leaned closer. Tab flinched as the manicured hand moved towards his neck. Try as he might, he couldn't stop his sphincter from releasing the hot liquid into his pants and down his legs. Luke's first touch was cool, the fingers like those of a masseuse...then the pain. Tab heard the bones and cartilage snapping and twisting in his neck. He clamped his healthy hand over Luke's in an attempt to pull it away. But Luke held firm. "Your voice is gone."

Tab gasped and tried to utter the words jumbling in his mind, but nothing came out coherent. A raspy, "Uh...uh...uh," floated into the air before he blacked out.

Tab McGrifth

33

Tab opened his eyes to a black, headlight lit road. He felt himself moving rapidly and blinked as he realized he was driving his Mercedes. His feet slammed on the brakes

Where am I?

He shook his head; tried to get his bearings. He gazed at the forest, the dark road, not feeling a bit of familiarity; no recollection of where he had been or should be. Suddenly he had the urge to look at his hands. He peered through the darkness at them. Knobby at the joints, pale, hairy, they were as normal as they'd ever been. He pulled the visor down and stared at his face. No changes visible there either.

My voice.

The thought frightened him. Tab took a deep breath and opened his mouth. "H…hell-o," he croaked, afraid for some reason he couldn't fathom. "Hello," he repeated, stronger. Confident now, he launched into his signature opening. "This is Tab McGrifth with 'Living Life As Your Right' on WJZU, FM 88.7." The tenor was smooth as molten lava.

Tab shook his head again then chuckled. "Must be that highway hypnosis," he muttered to himself. He pressed on the accelerator, his eyes straining for a road sign, street sign…something to jog his memory, let him know wherever he was. The fog obscured nearly everything beyond the car's beams. Then a name floated into his head: Luke.

Luke who? Something flitted just beyond his consciousness. A something that made shivers slither down his spine. His foot pressed harder on the accelerator.

Tab tried to relax and turned on the radio as the road unwound in front of him like a black ocean. The last coherent memory he could recall was his interview with Judge Hiram Hirsch. Contentment crept into his body as he remembered the interview—

"Shit!"

Tab swerved as the shape bounded in from the side. The car rocked as it glanced off his car. He saw hooves flash before the animal ran into the forest.

A deer. A damn deer.

Tab stopped the car. He wanted to assess the damage but then those hooves snap-flashed in his mind and his hand halted on the door release handle. They reminded him of…something. Something important.

He shook his head to clear it then rotated his neck a few times before checking the rearview mirror again and inching back down on the accelerator. His hands trembled on the steering wheel. Tab couldn't figure out why he was so jumpy. Why he felt apprehensive.

"You're losing it, old boy, you're losing it fast," he said to the air.

A sign appeared: I-92 ONE MILE. Tab grinned and gave the car more speed, glad to reach some place he was familiar with.

He rounded the curve too fast, eyes darting about looking for the exit ramp. Tab didn't see the little girl until she was in his beam. A curdling scream came from out of nowhere as the little brown face raced into focus. A pink mouth opened, eyes widened, hands moved up protectively. Tab tried to swerve; knew he was too late before he even made contact. A sickening bump…

Click.

#

The coffee aroma woke Tab. He opened his eyes to his treasured golden statue—The Princetown Radio Award—nearly touching the tip of his nose. Tab flipped upright, confusion masking his brain. Even more confusing was the light streaming in his window. He looked at his clock. Ten o'clock.

Had to be morning otherwise it'd be pitch black out. But why was he here at his desk at ten in the morning? His show wasn't on until four o'clock in the evening. Board meeting?

He looked around the room again before his shaky hands pulled his planner toward him. His eyes searched the page it was left open to: Thursday, January 12, 2006. Judge Hirsch's name was inked in for four o'clock. He'd remembered interviewing Judge Hirsch so today must be Friday. His fingers jerked from the book as his eyes read the name written in blue near the bottom of the page: Whitey Ford.

Snippets flashed in his head: Whitey asking for Jack Daniels; Whitey's gaunt appearance; Whitey probing into his past.

A knock sounded on the door. Before he could answer, in strode his secretary, Sheila. Sheila was a middle-aged widow who lived and breathed Tab and his show. Nothing was too much for him to ask her. Tab knew she'd had designs on him for years, but honestly, even though she was "well-preserved"—good legs, slim waist, good hair and makeup—she was still too old for his tastes.

"Thought I heard you moving around in here," Sheila said brightly, a cup of steaming coffee in her hands. "Black like you like it." She set the cup on the desk then asked, "Guess you're here because of the bad news, huh?"

Tab cocked an eyebrow and rubbed his forehead. "Bad news?"

Sheila swatted at him before answering. "Whitehall Fordham. Your old mentor?" Tab's pupils widened and his hand stilled. "Guess you heard the sons pulled the plug last night. Wife didn't want them to but they say he was having convulsions and fits like crazy!" Sheila shook her head. "Wonder what made that happen? You got any ideas?"

Whitey Ford. Tab's eyes drifted downward to the blue writing on the page. He saw Whitey's face clearly—the rheumy eyes, the hacking cough. Tab glanced up to see Sheila staring at him. He cleared his throat. "Uh, no. He'd been sick a long while."

"Really? I heard he'd just been admitted for some tests last week but he lapsed into a coma then onto brain dead before they got any results back. Probably cancer of the brain old as he was—"

The office door crashed open and in stepped two men dressed in dark suits with nearly identical buzz cuts. A uniformed police officer was behind them.

The one on the left barked, "Tab McGrifth?"

Tab stood, found his voice. "Yes?"

The one on the right stepped forward, a piece of paper in his hand. "You have the right to remain silent."

"What!" Both Tab and Sheila said simultaneously.

"Anything you say can and will be used against you in a court of law," the man continued.

"What's going on? What did I do?"

The man to the left stepped forward and held out the paper in his hand. "First of all, you are under arrest for prescription drug fraud."

The man to his right stopped his Miranda recitation and held out another sheet of paper. "Secondly, you are under arrest for vehicular homicide in the hit-and-run death of Angela Bofin."

"Wha…wha…?" Tab sputtered as the face of young girl—eyes wide in fear—zapped into his head.

The man on the right resumed reciting the Miranda rights. The man on the left signaled to the police officer. The officer stepped forward, a pair of handcuffs in his hands. Tab watched in slow motion as he brushed Sheila aside before he pulled his hands behind him and clasped the cuffs shut. Hands closed around his upper arm, propelled him towards the door.

"Wait!" Tab shouted. "Just wait one minute!" He twisted against the hands. They gripped him tighter and pushed him forward.

"I'll call Rob Thompson! He'll meet you down at the station!" Sheila called out to his back.

The flashes were blinding as he crossed the threshold.

Click.

#

"Tab. *Tab*," a voice repeated harshly.

Tab snapped to as Rob Thompson's narrow face swam into view. Rob's hair was slicked back and his suit spotless. His close set eyes, pointed nose and hairless face had always reminded Tab of a clean shaven rat. Tab looked around and realized he was in a courtroom.

Rob snapped his fingers under Tab's nose. "*Tab.* You've got to stay focused. You can't just blink out like that."

Tab's head spun but he managed to nod.

"Good. Now, do you want to accept the plea bargain?" Rob asked, eyes narrowed as he stared into Tab's face.

Tab searched for something familiar, something to remind him of...*something*. What had happened? What was Rob talking about? Why couldn't he remember? Not getting any answers in his head, he looked back at the staring Rob and said, "Remind me again of the charges and the plea."

Rob took a deep breath. "You can plead guilty to the vehicular homicide and take the two to ten sentence. You'll be out on the streets in three, five max." His hands animated for good measure.

Tab's memory of the three cops returned in a flash before Sheila's shocked face flipped into his head. He leaned back in his seat and crossed his arms. "And if I plead not guilty?"

Rob frowned. "You know how it goes. We do the whole shebang—risky trial and the sentence if convicted is ten to fifteen."

Tab shook his head. "I didn't do anything wrong."

Rob held a poker face as he said, "Her twelve year old brother got your tag number after the accident. There was blood on your Mercedes that matched Angela Bofin's. It was on the front fender in the dent on the bumper." Rob leaned in as he continued. "Tab, we don't want that twelve year old kid anywhere near the stand. You can't afford it. Kids make you believe them."

It wasn't a dream. I did hit that girl. Tab's mind searched for an alternative answer. "I remember a deer. It hit my car."

"So how did Angela's blood get there?"

Tab hung his head.

Rob sighed and laid his gold pen on the table. "Tab, we've been through all this. Do you want the deal or not? The prosecutor will work with us right now but if we wait, go to trial and that jury returns before we accept the plea or if the prosecution feels they are winning, all bets are off. Understand?"

Tab nodded.

"So what will it be?"

Click.

#

The pain in his side was intermittent but persistent. Tab clapped a hand over the offending area then jumped as he felt other flesh. *What the hell?* His eyes flipped open

"Wake up, motherfucka, time to toss some salad."

Tab's body stilled as rancid breath floated from a huge, dark shape less than a foot away. The voice was unfamiliar and the face not fully visible by the scant light available. A stiff finger poked his side again. Tab winced as he stared at the tattoos and muscles rippling down an enlarged arm.

I must be having a nightmare.

Tab surveyed the room quickly—concrete walls, no window and a stained commode and sink in the corner of the room. From the odor in the room, it had been recently used. He eyes skittered left and saw…bars.

Prison?

A hand closed around his neck and squeezed. "I started to pull your motherfucking ass out that damn bunk but I didn't wanna break your punk ass bones." The other hand—darkened further by tattoos or dirt, Tab couldn't tell—rubbed and squeezed the crotch inches from his face. "I got uses for yo' ass."

Tab instinctively pulled at the hands around his throat. The giant leaned his weight forward; Tab's windpipe narrowed significantly. He struck the arms, legs flailed searching for purchase.

The hulk ignored his movements; kept the pressure constant as he leaned his mouth inches from Tab's lips. Tab slapped at the face he now saw clearly—heavy Neanderthal forehead, one bushy eyebrow dividing the face, a twisted nose and thick lips beneath a pencil mustache. The head snapped back but the pressure on Tab's windpipe remained. "We can do this the easy way…or we can do this the hard way…but we *are* gonna do this." The man laughed low. "Hell, you might even enjoy it."

The hand released him. Tab gulped the stagnant air into his lungs; massaged his neck as he tried to understand where he was and what was actually happening. *Wake up! Damnit, wake up!* Tab slapped at his face; pinched his skin while the massive man watched and laughed.

"So you like it rough, huh?" Goliath said as he pulled his zipper down. Tab struggled to sit upright but years of good living and poor exercise habits hindered him. A hand pushed into his flabby chest and he flopped backwards. Tab watched in horror as Goliath shifted to the left and jiggled his legs before pulling his large penis free. "I like to give it rough, too." With that, he grabbed a handful of Tab's hair.

Tab screamed as his head was forced downward…

Chapter

34

Deva and Juan watched in horror as Tab melted to his knees, tears spewing from his eyes, guttural grunts and choked screams coming from his mouth.

Oh Lord, oh Lord, what is happening? Deva thought. Juan rubbed the rosary faster.

Luke watched, eyes glittering, a smile on his lips. As Tab clawed at his throat and mouth, he leaned forward. Both Juan and Deva took steps backwards.

"Tab. It's all right now," Luke said as he touched Tab's jerking head. "Come back. It's all over with."

Tab opened unfocused eyes, horror stamped in them. Luke touched him again. "You are here, in the present. Now."

Tab looked to his right at Deva and Juan. Amazingly, a smile split his lips. He rose awkwardly and clasped his hands in front of him. "A dream! Tell me it was a dream!" he whisper-rasped as he walked towards Deva and Juan.

"You're correct. It was a dream…now," Luke interrupted. "But it is the reality awaiting you if you don't meet the conditions of our initial contract."

"Wh..what?" The sandpaper voice grated nerves as he spun his head around to include Luke. "What do you mean?"

Luke sucked his teeth. "Think of it like the Ghost of Christmas Future. What you saw is what awaits you if you don't join the Kingdom as promised."

Tab's face fell. Tears welled in his lids. He cleared his throat repeatedly to no avail. He finally croaked, "You mean..."

"Exactly."

Tab crumbled to the floor, yowling at pain only he and Luke knew about.

Luke watched Tab disinterestedly before he eyed Deva for a moment then moved to her. Deva cringed, her body screaming for her to run but she was immobile. Luke's hands grasped the sides of her head and lingered. "Ahh, the beauteous Deva. What heights we have soared to." Luke's hands stroked her lover-like and his eyes softened as he surveyed her from head to toe. "The voice, the look, the body." As he completed this sentence, his hands pressed inwards.

Deva's head felt like it was being split open. A headache thundered in her skull and her face burned as if a scorching pan had been placed on it. She smelled the flesh burning, the smoke thick as she inhaled it through her pain. Her lungs screamed in agony in their search for clean air. But Luke held firm as the bolts of pain surged from her head, down her throat and lower still. She felt things shifting, contracting, stretching. Her back twisted then bowed, knees buckled but Luke held on.

He finally released her and stood back looking her up and down. "Girl, you're not looking *nearly* as good as you use to!" Luke mimed a woman's voice then threw back his head and guffawed.

Deva felt trapped in the mangled body; wanted to run but the new limitations of her grotesqueness hindered her. Wanted to scream but choked it back as she saw Luke's body shift. She tensed. Waited for…whatever.

Luke leaned forward until his sulphorous breath bathed her face. "Same deal. See what kind of life awaits you, my dear."

Deva

35

The noise was deafening as the music thumped, the crowd yelled.

Where am I? Deva looked down the well-lit hallway and the metal stairwell at the end. The music was louder there. The instruments suddenly took it down a couple of decibels and she heard the crowd chanting, "De-va! De-va! De-va!"

Okay, a concert. But where? She lifted a foot and froze. *I shouldn't be able to walk.* Deva looked down at her sandal-clad feet. The silver nail polish twinkled back at her in the light. She wriggled her toes. They worked fine.

She was staring at her straight legs when Lena clacked down the stairwell. "What are you waiting on! You're up now! You don't want Jimmy Tomahawk to steal your show, do you?"

Jimmy Tomahawk? She'd had a conversation about him recently…but with whom? And what was he doing at her concert? She'd no more invite Jimmy to sing at her concert than she would Ed Burris.

Ed.

A frisson of fear raced down her back as images of a smiling Ed unlocked themselves from her memory. Her heart thudded, skin crawled.

"Are you coming?" Lena said, head peeping down the stairwell as she yelled to Deva. She frowned before she straightened and skipped the rest of the way to the floor. "What's wrong? What happened?" Her eyes darted all around for trouble.

"N…nothing," Deva whispered, skin clammy, eyes wide. "I'm fine."

"No, you are *not* fine." Lena felt her head. "You're cold as ice. I don't understand. You were okay ten minutes ago. Did something happen in the dressing room?" Ed's face flashed in Deva's head and she winced. "What is it?"

"I…I don't know." Deva shook her head. "It's nothing. Nothing."

"Uh uh. There is definitely something wrong here," Lena asserted as she pressed Deva against the wall. "Spill it."

Ed's face cameoed again then a name: Luke. The name made her body shake; made the room spin. The visible trembling had Lena yelling, "Cayman! Cayman, come quick!"

A door opened behind them and running steps were heard. "What wrong with you, girl? You just about made me have a heart attack!" Cayman yelled as he turned the corner, running on his tip toes. "This better be—" Cayman stopped his prancing as he spotted the still-quaking Deva.

"Something is wrong with Deva!"

"Yeah." Cayman lifted her head, all male now. "Deva! Look at me!" No response. "Deva!" he screamed.

Deva focused on the voice as the world around her righted. *What was that?*

"Deva? Can you hear me, girlfriend?" Cayman yelled in her face.

Cayman's frightened face swam into view. Deva swatted at him. "Yes! And would you please stop yelling at me." Lena and Cayman exchanged looks. "I'm fine. I just felt out of sorts for a moment. I'm fine right now."

Lena stared as she rubbed Deva's arms. Cayman took a step backwards and twirled a finger before landing it on his hip, girlie-girl back in play. "Alright. In that case, you'd better get your butt on stage 'cause Jimmy Tomahawk is about to steal *your* show."

Click.

#

The persistent knocking woke her. Deva opened her eyes to a hotel suite. Toile tapestry hung from rods around the round bed she was lying on. As she parted the curtain of material, she saw a sitting area with a chaise lounger and ottoman to her right. A large flat screened television played muted videos on the wall in front of her. The carpet was deep enough to lose an earring in.

Where am I? She didn't remember ever having visited so plush of a suite before on tour and she'd visited many.

The knocking became pounding.

"I'm coming! I'm coming!"

Deva pulled the sheets back and realized she was naked beneath. She swung her feet to the floor surprised when she heard a crackle under her foot. She looked down, was shocked to see men's briefs on the floor and as she shifted her foot, the condom wrapper beside them.

What the—?

Deva then realized the shower was running and glanced at the bathroom door. *Who the hell?*

The knocks boomed now. She pushed the briefs and running shower from her mind as she looked for a robe. "I'm coming!" Seeing nothing, she pulled the sheet from the bed and wrapped it around her frame. Before she reached the door, she heard voices then a key inserted into the lock. *Must be Lena or Cayman.*

She turned back, deciding she needed to know just who was in her shower then she'd deal with her staff.

She never got the chance.

"Where is he? Where is my baby? You're not gonna do him like this again!"

Deva swung around and saw a red-lipsticked, helmet-haired woman screeching at her—Maria Tomahawk. People fanned out around her, cameras flashing.

Shit! It must be Jimmy in the shower!

She slammed the bedroom door and locked it. The pounding on the door started up moments later. "Open this door, you child molester! My Jimmy is underage! Open this door or I'm calling the police!"

Jimmy had turned eighteen and they both knew it. But she knew the press didn't care. A story was a story and this was a doozy of one. Deva sprinted to the closed bathroom door—*My God! Can't he hear the commotion?*— and threw it open.

She screamed loud and long as she watched the naked body revolving in midair.

Click.

#

"Bitch, you got my money?" A stinging slap followed the question.

Deva's face slammed into the ground. She tasted dirt and smelled dog crap. Her head lifted just as a foot stomped on her back. "Owww!"

"Bitch, you heard me the first time. You got my money?" *What was he talking about? Who was this?* "Oh, now you want to play dumb?" Another stomp.

"Wait! Wait!" Deva screamed and rolled onto her hips. Blood dribbled from her lips; her back was on fire. *What was going on?* A skinny Hispanic man with spiked black hair and sunglasses stood over her.

"I don't need to wait. I told you the last time we talked I needed my money. Now you got the money or what?" he snarled then spat on the ground beside her.

Deva's head jerked as she looked at her surroundings—garbage-strewn street, buildings with graffiti on them and a chain link fence beside her. *This must be a bad dream.*

"Oh, cat got your tongue?" The foot lifted again.

Her heart lurched. "Money!" she screamed. "I can get your money! I've got plenty of it!"

The foot lowered to the ground. The man took off his sunglasses. A jagged cut ran from the middle of his forehead, across his nose and ended in a wide scar at his cheek. A tattoo of tears ran from the scar and below the collar of his shirt. The eyes flashed as he knelt to where she was. "Really?"

"Y…yes! I'm Deva! I have money!"

The man's head snapped back as he opened his mouth and laughed loudly. "*You* have money. The infamous *Deva* has money?"

Infamous? "Yes, I have money."

The laughter cut off like a faucet. "Where is it then? My man had a *friendly* talk with your accountant today and we only found one hundred and fifty seven thousand in the bank." Deva was stunned. She had millions. "Also…you have no offshore accounts, your stocks have been liquidated and your houses sold. Wrongful death lawsuits are a motha! Of course your 'Dream Team' of lawyers didn't cut you any slack either. I bet you wish Johnny were still around, don't cha?" The lethal light brown eyes stared at her as the serpentine neck elongated and head cocked to the side. "So tell me…where is this money?" He rubbed the scar.

Something happened between me and Jimmy Tomahawk. Deva's mind spun in confusion but she tried to stay focused on the situation at hand. She'd sort out the Jimmy thing later. "I…I can get it."

The man snorted. "Bitch, we talked about what would happen if you didn't make good on the half-million I fronted you."

Half a million dollars? Him?

'Let me remind you again. The interest is one hundred percent per month. At this point you now owe me three million dollars and the penalty, if you can't pay Glock now, will be one ugly sonofabitch." Deva's eyes were saucers. Glock. What type of name was that? Her pondering was cut short as the man now known as Glock grabbed her chin, dug his long manicured nails into her jaw flesh and cheek. Light glinted off the clear nail polish, flashed as his index finger punctuated ever word. "You thought I was playing or something?"

This is real. Glock is real. "N…no. I didn't think you were playing."

"Seems to me you thought so," Glock huffed, sucking at his teeth. "I anticipated that. Bring her around, Fred!" he barked.

Muffled voices then the sounds of a struggle were heard. The man lifted and stared behind him. "Can't you handle that old biddie, Fred?"

Fred. What a man, what a man, what a huge ass mighty big man. Fred was lineman material—tall, broad shoulders and muscles from head to toe. He'd make any woman feel safe when she was with him; make any man pause before issuing an unarmed challenge.

Fred currently struggled with a woman who was giving him fits. The woman—Deva strained but couldn't tell much about her in the declining light—scratched and swatted at his face until he finally picked her up and tossed her over his shoulder. He dumped her at Glock's feet. She lifted her head revealing a very familiar face.

"Mama!" Deva screamed and lifted to her knees. A backhand slap slung her into the fence.

"Sit yo' ass down!"

Deva stared at her dishelved mother—dress torn, hair standing up on her head and ripped pantyhose—so far from normal, regular. Right now, her mother strongly resembled Phyllis Diller on a bad acid trip.

"Baby, it's all right. I'm fine," Mama said in her it's-gonna-be-all-right voice.

"You think so?" Glock sneered. He opened his jacket and pulled a gun out. Deva held her breath as Glock spat, squatted next to her. His voice was caressing as he asked, "So, what's it gonna be? Money…" Deva's heart solidified into a block of ice as he swung the gun slowly away from her and towards her mother. "...or Mama?"

Deva's heart thumped; tears gushed. This Glock person was crazy! Just crazy! "No! I'll get you the money! Don't hurt my mother!"

Glock shook his head and rolled his eyes. "Too late for that. I repeat, money or Mama." Glock took a step closer to Deva's mother; held the gun to her head.

"I don't know what's happened but I swear to you, I'll get the money! Please! Just a little more time! I can raise the cash! Please."

"Don't worry about me, baby. I've lived my time." Deva's mother's eyes were moist but her tone was soothing. Deva didn't feel soothed one bit.

"That's what I thought." The man said as he cocked the pistol.

Deva surged from the ground, fear making her bold. "Wait! I told you I could get—"

The retort of the gun was deafening…

Chapter 36

"Noooo! God, no!" Deva wailed. Tab stared; Juan whispered a prayer as he massaged the rosary in his pocket. "Please God, not my mother! Please God!"

Suddenly, the earth groaned and shook. The walls behind Luke crumbled away and flames shot through. Heat and sulfur suffused the room. The sound of howls, growls and barks was incredible.

"Come!" Luke yelled as his face morphed—the horns, the clawed hands and hooves, the scales—then the sound of feet marching, hundreds or thousands of feet marching forward.

But first…the snakes came.

They poured over the crumbled concrete—iridescent, red, black, green, striped, fat, skinny, short and long—hissing and slithering onto chairs, tables and towards the four people.

"No! Ggg!" Tab grunted and turned. "Jesus help us!" Deva screamed and skittered backwards on her crippled legs. "Dios! Run!" Juan yelled and lifted the shuffling Deva from the floor before twisting to flee. Luke lifted a scaled finger, freezing them mid-stride.

The snakes kept coming. They crawled and slid up legs, around waists, across chests, inside clothes and finally flicked tongues on faces. Tears dripped down immobilized flesh; screams suffocated in paralyzed vocal chords. Breath held in lungs; hearts arrythmatic in chests.

Their eyes watched as fire, intense, flash-melting fire, cleared the path for the unknown. Smaller snakes curled and vaporized as the flames moved inside the building. Eyes stretched further at the sight of rotting bodies and eyeless sockets dripping maggots marching two by two. The larger snakes slithered towards the dead mass, curled around and inside skeletal remains; displaced shredded flesh and maggots.

The lead...*thing*...had one leaking eye bulging from its socket and foot-long fangs protruding past curling, half-rotted lips. A chain was wrapped around naked hand bones, the end attached to an enormous three-headed pit bull. The dog was pony-sized and its feet scraped the ceiling as it lunged and snapped at the air. The dog's teeth were pointed, the claws, talons.

Luke's obsidian eyes peered at Deva; claws grasped and pulled her face upwards. The twisted body protested. Malodor shot up her nose as his face met hers. "If I hear *His* name one...more...time, you will *all* have to contend with Cerberus!" Luke thundered, spittle spray sizzling her skin. The dog strained at its chain, snarled and barked at them as if confirming this fact. The snakes hissed in unison.

Luke held onto Deva's face as he pried Juan's hands away. The snakes slid up his arms and around his head, swaying. Deva thought her neck would snap as Luke lifted and plopped her on a snake-covered chair. The reptilian creatures covered her head, obscured her fright-widened eyes. The oblong heads struck over and over but stopped just before contact with flesh.

Juan's trapped scream tried mightily to be released as he watched Luke's eyes train upon him. He willed his legs to move, thought he felt a muscle contraction when—

"It's no use, Juan," Luke said as he grasped Juan's unburnt hand. Juan could only watch in horror as his skin and the entrapped snakes bubbled, split then burst open, splattering them both.

Noooooo! Juan screamed in his head. The remaining snakes retreated upwards and downwards, blinding and binding Juan as Luke held on. The tendons contracted, pulling the bones backwards until they were bent over Juan's wrist. A snake's body shifted in time for Juan to see Luke scrape burned tissue from his scaled hand and sniff. Luke's nostrils quivered. "Just like home," he said before he flicked his tongue out, captured the flesh… chewed.

Juan's eyes rotated in his head but righted as he felt Luke's talons enter his chest and drag downwards. The snakes circling his head dropped away as Luke leaned in. "Your turn, my man. Enjoy."

Juan Rodriquez

37

Screeeeeeeech. Screeeeeeech. Screeeeeeeech. Screeeeeech.

The constant whine made Juan open his eyes. Dials glowed inches from his face. Startled, he pushed backward. It was then he realized he was sitting in his car. In front of his house. The wipers screeched across the dry windshield again. Juan silenced them and rubbed his chin.

I don't remember driving home.

But there it stood, 1145 Maple Avenue, an impressive brick Tudor with a four car garage. Loam's toy Humvee was parked next to the entrance where he always left it. Loam said he felt like a superstar when he could pull up to the door.

Juan's hand shook violently as he reached for the door handle. He stared at the quivering flesh as the fingers jerked erratically and muscles contracted involuntarily. *What's wrong with me?*

His thought was interrupted when the front door opened and Zeus sprinted across the lawn towards him. Juan noticed the scowl on the handsome face just as Zeus snatched the door open and shouted, "Where the hell have you been!" Juan blinked and pulled his head backwards, unable to answer. "Oh, now you can't talk?" Zeus thrust his head inside the car and twisted Juan's shirt in his hands. "I said, where have you been? It sure as hell wasn't *Zinzibaz*!" Zeus snarled.

Juan and Zeus never fought. Zeus' easygoing demeanor and stable personality is what attracted Juan to him in the first place. It was not evident now. Juan swallowed as he stared into Zeus' hard eyes.

"I...I...was—" *Where the hell* had *he been?* No clue popped into his head.

Zeus tightened his grip on the shirt and screamed, "Out with some new trade? You lied to me to get with some new action? All the time we've invested in this relationship and you lie and sneak out the house to get with some new man?" The spittle sprayed into the air.

"No! I haven't been with—" Bodie's face flashed in his mind and he faltered. *Bodie? What the hell is Bodie doing in my head? I'm done with that.*

"You can't even say it yourself. Who was it?" Zeus held on as he pierced Juan's soul with his eyes.

Juan shook his head. "No. I wasn't with anyone. Promise."

Zeus searched his face another minute. Juan prayed he didn't see some truth he wasn't aware of. Zeus finally sighed before releasing Juan and leaning out the car. "Okay. You say you haven't been with anyone...so where *have* you been?" He tapped his foot on the driveway concrete.

"I...was..." Juan tried to remember but nothing came to mind. "I was supposed to go to *Zinzibaz* but...I saw Erlich before I got there." Erlich, a mutual friend, was safe—sixty-five, wheelchair bound and straight as an arrow. Nevertheless, Juan resolved to call him so their stories matched.

Zeus' face changed. Calm again. "Oh."

"So why were you looking for me?"

"It's four o'clock in the morning. Why *wouldn't* I be looking for you?" Zeus narrowed his eyes again. "What were you and old Erlich doing all this time?"

Juan pulled his legs out the car and stood. He had no idea what he'd been doing for the past eight hours but he'd begun the lie so he planned to finish it on a high note. "Oh you know how lonely Erlich is. I listened to his old 45's as he talked about his life 'before.'"

Erlich's car accident had left him a paraplegic but his wife's departure had left him a mental cripple. Anything that occurred prior to her zooming away in her Honda, leaving Erlich a total wreck, was 'before.' Juan stretched and was rewarded with popping bones.

"What's that?" Zeus asked, staring at Juan's feet.

"Huh?" Juan's fogged mind didn't understand the question.

Zeus pointed to the ground. Juan followed his finger and saw the small box illuminated by the interior car light. Juan inhaled sharply as a vision of Bodie, holding an identical box, flashed in his head. He felt Zeus watching him closely. His mouth went dry as he slowly reached for the box.

"What's in the box, Juan?" Zeus said, excitement tingeing his voice.

Juan already knew he knew the contents. *Lord, why now?* Yes, he loved Zeus...but enough to marry him? Even though he'd been the same sex marriage agenda's biggest promoter, it wasn't *right.* Not by God. Deep down, not by him. But what to do?

"Juan?" Zeus' voice was heavy with expectancy.

Juan looked at the joy-restrained face; came up with no good options. If he brushed it off, there was a pouting Zeus to contend with and life would probably get sticky. If he followed the expected path, there was…He shook his head. With a sigh, he went down on one knee. He lifted his heavy, pounding head, and with an even heavier heart said, "Zeus, will you do me the honor of marrying me?"

Zeus squealed in two octaves as Juan snapped the lid open revealing a sparkling band he wished were in someone else's hands.

Click

#

A tugging on his coat got his attention. Juan stared at his own reflection in the mirror and was shocked to see he was wearing a tuxedo, a top of the line, double breasted, stiff neck, bowtie demanding, cummerbund requiring tuxedo…and Loam was frantically pulling on his coattail. Loam's eyes darted behind him as he tugged again.

Juan turned from the mirror and leaned down on one knee before pulling Loam to him. He felt Loam's little body shaking and he shifted him backwards, tilted his face to his.

"What's wrong, Loam?"

Loam twisted his head to look behind him as he surged back into Juan's arms.

Juan looked around and realized they were in a bathroom. A public bathroom.

Where are we?

He pulled Loam off his shoulder. He was stunned to see tears rolling down his face. "What's wrong, Loam? Tell Daddy what's wrong."

Loam sniffled and shook but no sound exited his miniature mouth. Juan had never seen him like this. His happy baby scared. Fear simmered in his stomach. He tried to maintain calm as he asked, "Did something happen to Zeus?"

Loam shook his head.

"What's wrong then? It can't be all that bad." *Yes it can. It can be way worse than you think.*

Juan flinched at the unbidden message. Fear niggled at his tailbone and crept, oozed steadily up his back. He pushed down on his flash fear and focused on Loam. "Son, look at me. Tell me what's wrong so I can fix it," Juan insisted.

With tears pouring down his face, Loam lifted his head an inch, eyes averted downward and whispered, "Am I a queerbaby?"

Juan's head snapped up; his mind reeled in indignation. This question eventually had to be answered but he'd hoped he had at least five more years before actually addressing it. He kept his voice neutral as he asked, "Where did you hear that?"

"Daddy, he'll hear you," Loam whispered, fear evident in his features as he gave a quick look behind him.

Juan looked past Loam and saw nothing out of the ordinary—stalls with open doors, ceramic all over the place. Except for them, the room was empty. He turned back to Loam. "Who? Who said something like that?"

Loam's body shook as he looked toward the closed entrance door again. "The man by the door said I was a queerbaby and you and Daddy were big queers…" he turned and glanced at the door again, "and mean, old Luke was gonna burn me up because I was a queerbaby." He flew back into Juan's arms.

Luke. The name made Juan shake for some reason. He swallowed bitter bile; forced down the urge to sling open a stall and spew his guts out as the name reverberated in his head. *Luke.* The walls seemed to inch inward. The light streaming in dimmed.

Juan had to get out of there. He picked up Loam and on jelly legs strode across the ceramic tiles. Just as he reached for the handle, his hand faltered as a face appeared in the stainless door plate…brown, familiar. He immediately knew: This was *Luke.*

Fear squeezed his innards as Loam seemed to convulse; hold him tighter, face scrunched between his shoulder and neck. As he stared at the image, the mouth parted and smiled…as the eyes glowed.

Juan's heart lurched, "God, be with me" fell unbidden from his lips. The face frowned, eyes elongated. Puffs of smoke curled from the wide nostrils. Juan watched as the smoke traversed the only-my-imagination plane and wisped into the room.

"Daddy, something stinks," Loam whispered, face still nestled under Juan's neck.

My God, what's happening here? Juan broke eye contract and grasped the door handle. It was surprisingly cool. He snatched it open and surged across the threshold. Someone jostled him from the side. Juan swung around, heart nearly stopping as he saw the light brown face.

"Sorry, son. You alright?" the older woman asked.

Juan stared, immobilized by fear and skin color.

"You okay? I didn't hurt you and your queerbaby, did I?"

Juan's heart double-clutched, arms tightened around Loam. "What did you just say?" he whispered.

"I said, I didn't hurt you and your dear baby, did I?" The woman repeated. Juan was about to reply when the woman smiled…revealing rows of metal fangs.

Juan yelped as his heart stuttered then hammered in his chest. He felt powerless to move as the woman leaned closer, her now fetid breath washing across his face. "Luke said to tell you and the *queerbaby* hello."

Click.

#

"Burn, faggots, burn! Burn, faggots, burn!" The chant grew louder and more forceful.

Juan realized he was standing on a platform, a crowd of people, some carrying placard with antihomosexual slogans on them, others with Gay Pride in bold letters, below him chanting.

"Burn, faggots, burn!"

"Gay love is as good as any other love!"

"Juan! Juan!" Zeus hissed behind him, "Go ahead with your speech."

Juan tried to focus, tried to understand why he was there. What had the crowd so animated. He tilted his head backwards, covered the microphone inches from him mouth and whispered to Zeus, "I lost my train of thought. What was I saying?"

Zeus wrinkled his eyebrows before answering, "This is a Pro Same Sex Marriage rally. How could you forget? Are you alright?"

Juan didn't answer as he swiveled back to the mic, ready to ad lib on his pet topic. He cleared his voice before speaking. "Same sex marriage is *not* an abomination. It is the same institution as heterosexual marriage."

Boos and hisses rang throughout the crowd. The 'Burn, faggot, burn' chant resumed louder this time.

Juan waited for the comments to settle. His eyes roamed the crowd noting the usual myriad of characters at these types of rallies—college students, housewives, men in work clothes and of course, the clergy. As he swung his head for another survey, a young man caught his eye. Or rather, the actions of a young man caught his eye.

The kid was blond, lanky…a dead ringer for Bodie. *And* he was stroking himself. Not through his pants. He held his erect penis in his hand; was stroking it as he watched Juan. No one else seemed to notice the kid. He was ignored as the taunts continued.

Juan felt his mouth go dry as his penis stiffened.

"Go ahead, Juan," Zeus urged behind him.

Juan dragged his eyes away and focused on the middle of the crowd. "Loving someone of the same sex is not a perversion. It is—" Juan faltered as his eyes were drawn back to the kid as he spit into his hand before running it up and down his lengthening shaft.

You know you want it, the kid mouthed.

Juan heard the silky voice he knew so well as if he were next to him instead of thirty feet away. *Definitely* Bodie. Juan couldn't stop staring at this young Bodie clone, at what the kid was doing because, if the erection now tenting his pants was any indication, damn if he didn't want him…as he always had.

Juan cleared his throat again and tried to remember what he was saying. "Same sex love is just like any other loving relationship. We want families. We want companionship. We want—" *You want to sink your cock in my hot ass and pump like there is no tomorrow,* the Bodie clone teased.

Juan shook his head, tried to clear the thought away. "We want intimate, trusting love. Love like—" *What I can give you. Come get it,* the kid taunted, spreading his legs, leaning backwards, stroking in earnest.

As Juan saw the drop of precum glistening at the tip of the kid's member, memories of another love, another time suffused his brain and he forgot where he was as he sighed, "Bodie," into the microphone.

"What the fuck does a 'love like Bodie' mean?" Zeus screeched behind him.

Click

#

The dream was too real, too vivid.

The room was small and cramped. A desk sat in the corner covered with papers and books. Moonlight shined on clothes draped across chairs. It had been years but Juan knew this room well. It was the old bedroom he'd had shared with Bodie. Juan wanted to pinch himself…but he wanted to see where the dream took him too bad to wake up.

The body next to him shifted, oh so familiar hands roamed across his abdomen before tangling into his bush. Juan's body turned to liquid as the hand teased and pulled at his pubic strands. He felt his member stirring, elongating as practiced fingers brushed lightly along its length.

Juan had always been the giver and rarely the receiver so he lay motionless as the sheet tented before a tongue flicked into his navel. Juan's toes curled as the appendage rotated in and out of his sensitive zones, nipped at his lower belly flesh. His body clenched as the tongue moved lower, followed the path of prior hands through his pubic hair. He sighed as a hand stroked his stiff pole before warm breath flitted along the length of it. Then…the tongue licked him.

Juan unhinged. Dream merged with reality as he tangled his hands in hair, surged into the hot wetness. The mouth was small, tight, and hotter than anything he'd remembered. He pumped forcefully, refusing to allow the hot orifice he rarely felt to unseat from his member. Felt the glorious testosterone swimming in his bloodstream; felt his pole engorge more as he hit the back of the throat. Juan couldn't hold back, could stop himself as his balls tightened in their sac. He cried to the ceiling as his juice spewed from his pole.

The light was flicked on. "What's wrong?" Zeus shouted, hands clutched to his chest.

Juan's eyes flipped open simultaneously banishing the too real dream and slamming him back into reality. That's when Juan realized that indeed he held hair in his hands and his penis was enclosed in a mouth, the wetness running down and between his legs. *Oh shit!*

Zeus noticed the other lump in the bed. "What the hell is this?" he yelled as he snatched the sheets away that covered Juan and the person with him.

Horror rendered them both mute as the light revealed Loam, tears streaming down his face, vomitus and semen spilling from his mouth…

Chapter

38

The keening, sorrow-filled wail emitting from Juan lifted the hair on Deva and Tab. They could only stare as Juan's chest heaved and a tear/snot mixture ran in rivulets down his face.

"Not a pretty picture, was it?" Luke cackled. Cerberus barked and an unholy cacophony of sounds emitted from his dead army.

Luke's eyes swept over them slowly, thoroughly before he barked, "Enough of these games. Time for some answers." He snapped his fingers twice. The fire disappeared, the army, snakes and dog backed into the hole in the wall, the concrete blocks closing off their entrance.

Luke shrank, morphed once again to his white suited, African American form. "Now kids, you know the deal." He held their gaze. His essence reached, pulled, searched for an opening into their floundering souls. Not finding an easy, willing capitulation, Luke shrugged, gave them a chaste smile. "Hey, I know I made it seem bad but believe me," his eyes narrowed, "that was only the preview. The reality is way, way worse."

Luke stood, walked toward Deva. She tried to shrink further into her seat but was unable. His fingers caressed her face lightly from eye to chin before clasping around her neck. He leaned forward. Deva felt the hands around her neck. "Noooooo!" she screamed with all her might over and over again.

Luke ignored the screams as his hands tightened beneath her chin. "This won't hurt a bit," he assured her and pulled upwards. Deva's screams became howls as her body untwisted, muscles unknotted, stretched back to normal. Luke kept the pressure on as he lifted her from the chair to her original form. "See, right as rain."

"B…but I don't understand. What's going on?" Deva stuttered. *Had Luke changed his mind?*

Luke pressed a finger to her lips. "Shhh. Just wait."

With that Luke turned towards Juan. Snot had gelled on Juan's face. Luke didn't hesitate instead he grasped Juan's deformed hand. Juan hiccupped as he watched the tendons and ligaments snaking into the air before finding their corresponding bones and muscles. The tears stopped as the skin regenerated over the open tissue. Luke slapped him on the shoulder, "You took it like a *real* man," then laughed hysterically at his own joke.

As Juan stood flexing his hand, Luke moved on to Tab. He grasped Tab's hair and pulled him forward. Tab gurgled something incoherent. Luke ignored him as he slid his hand down Tab's face and to his throat. Tab felt the bones shifting, pushing, realigning beneath Luke's hot fingers. As he released Tab, Luke said, "You're lying tongue works again, my friend."

"I don't understand. Have you changed your mind?" Deva questioned, hopeful that this was truly a bad dream, that Luke was just a figment of her imagination and she'd wake up soon.

Luke spun around, his eyes blazing. "On the contrary. I want you all to be fully able to answer. No mumbling and saying 'you didn't mean it'; I misunderstood. I want to be able to hear you when you say 'Yes.'

"So what will it be folks?" Luke looked expectantly from one to the other.

Deva deflated, felt as though she'd lived a lifetime this evening. And even though the images of her future were horrifying, she was more determined than ever that if she had to die, she would die with the words of God on her lips. *You've got to stand for something,* her mother always said. She squared her trembling shoulders.

Luke saw. "I see you want to be first, Deva." Luke held out his hand. "Will you join my Kingdom?"

Deva took a deep breath then faltered as visions pushed into her head. She saw images of her mother, brain splattered on the pavement; saw Jimmy Tomahawk swinging in the hotel room; Hank Swazy standing beside her, chest puffed out proudly as he stood backstage with her after a concert; saw the succession of now forgotten, nameless hard bodies in every color of skin stroking, biting and licking as she writhed in ecstasy beneath them, shame filling her as she watched her own wanton behavior; wondered if she could live life with no money and being *infamous.*

The verdict was there: Cafeteria Christian. She would tell anybody she was a Christian but in reality she was living like she wanted to and taking and twisting The Word to ease her conscious about her activities. But that's all she'd known: Do what you want six days and on the seventh be cleansed when you showed up for church. Is that what she meant? No and God knew she didn't. She'd fallen but grace and mercy was still there for the asking. She said a silent prayer as the images flashed over and over, more horrifying each time.

Deva knew her life would never be the same no matter the choice she made. So be it. Her body quaked but she pushed the fear down. She wasn't willing or truly able to turn her back on what was her spiritual grounding despite how far away she'd strayed. There was no comparison with what God offered and this spawn standing in front of her promised in his Kingdom.

With a heavy heart, she lifted her eyes to the demon king, the consummate liar, deceiver, the beguiling entity who'd ensnared and entrapped her, playing on her fears, her anxieties, her frustrations and now stood promising her tomorrow knowing he wouldn't allow her to live past today. Deva pushed around the panic bubbling, asking to be released from her controlled mind, swallowed the dread, the repulsion now living and pulsing within her and said in a shaky, trembling but yet, still strong voice, "I claim the Kingdom of God!" The voice thundered and bounced within the room.

The building began shaking violently. The floorboards lifted and tilted. They were all thrown to the floor, clutching at tables and chairs as the earth groaned and rumbled leaving a cavernous hole belching flames in the center of the floor. Deva and Tab scrambled backwards on one side, Juan on the other.

Luke hissed, "You dare defy me! After all this? After I've shown you your future, you dare to say *His* name to my face?" His hands swept towards her fallen form. "Be as you were!"

Deva screamed as the pain returned multiplied by five. Visions of her old pastor standing in the pulpit screaming damnation at the backsliders branded her brain as her back screeched as it bowed, muscles twisted, legs bent. "God, no! God, no!" Her elbows folded into unnatural angles; her head turned against her might nearly strangling her, making her gasp for air.

The hole in the floor widened as Tab crawled towards the contorting Deva. Luke crossed the space, walking on the leaping flames, and hovered just at the edge of the hole. His maddened eyes blazed red. "Tab, this is your chance to be as glorious in my Kingdom as you have been here on Earth. To sit as the Prince of Hades; serve as my right-hand man. What do you say?"

Though he heard the question, Tab never ceased crawling until he reached Deva. He ignored the heat searing up his back, blanked Luke from his mind as he cradled Deva's twisted head. Honestly, he didn't know why he'd done it. He'd never been fond of Blacks but there was something about seeing a woman, any woman, screaming in pain he just couldn't accept; a wrongness that couldn't be ignored.

The burned wig fell off in his hands. He pushed it from Deva's shoulders as he tried to position her more comfortably. "It's gonna be alright, Deva. It's gonna be alright," he said soothingly.

"Tab, answer me, dammit!" Luke rumbled menacingly.

Tab still felt the bile sloshing in his stomach, still remembered the horror awaiting him if he answered no. But hell, the torments of Hell were way worse than any lawsuit, lack of money or being rammed up the rear. Besides, he was no Bible scholar as much as he'd like to portray himself as one. The success didn't allow him time to frolic with common folk. But he did remember something Deva had said earlier: God didn't work like this. Not this can't find redemption, live in Hell forever for a mistake stuff. For all his sins, he knew he'd never blasphemed God. He may have wished something crazy once upon a time, but it was just that, a foolish wish.

Blood sang in Tab's ears as he trained his tired eyes on the human cloaked monster in front of him, opened his mouth and said as loud as he could, "I choose God!"

Luke flew to Tab, snatched him to his chest, levitating them over the fire pit. The heat was nearly unbearable to Tab. He flailed his legs and arms, felt his shoes melting away, smelled his hair smoldering.

Luke leaned in, lips millimeters from Tab's mouth. Tab shuddered as...*things* moved behind Luke's eyes. "You would deny me? Your *Master*?" The sulfurous breath sucked the air from Tab's lungs. "You would rather be a punk ass fairy than to reign tall in my Kingdom? Would you?"

Tab refused to break eye contact; knew that he'd have no other chance to prove himself. "I...choose...God!"

Luke flung Tab from him. Tab screamed, arms wind-milled as he dove toward the liquid death. Juan and Deva's screams echoed Tab's. As the flames leaped around him, Tab prayed for divine intervention, prayed for a ledge, prayed for anything to give him a chance at saving himself. He twisted his body, realized there were no sides, only fire below.

A succession of images played across his eyes—his meek mother and onerous father; Whitey Ford at his peak and his recent frail state; Rosaparks Simpson naked and crying in a hotel room, questions of love flowing from her mouth; women he'd used without a thought, taking what they'd given eagerly well aware they had higher expectations he had no plans of offering; other people he'd stepped on in his quest for success. Tears formed and were quickly evaporated as the truth of his life was revealed. The lies. The deceit. Tab finally did what he'd always faked, never found the conviction within himself to do before: He prayed earnestly for forgiveness.

The closer Tab got to the flames, the more unbearable the heat became. His face burned; nerve endings pulsated like a thousand jack hammers. His clothes burst into flames; he was in excruciating pain all over. Just as Tab realized there was no saving himself, he let out one last shout, "Gooood! I believeeeee!" and just like that, an angel seemed to float upwards and open its arms right before he splashed into the molten fire.

Tab squinted at the bright light, the arms surrounding him. He stared at the golden wings encasing him and then up to the face, the beauteous face smiling at him. "Let me take you to the true Master." Tab could only nod. The flames dissipated as the world as he knew it disappeared.

"*Dios! Dios!* How could you!" Juan was hysterical. "How could you! How could you just drop him into the fire like that? The deal was that we either go with you or suffer hell on Earth, right?"

"You changed the rules on me so now I've changed the rules on you!" Luke snarled. "I've been as patient as I'm going to be here."

"B…but—"

Luke cut Juan off. "No more questions! It's time for my answer! Either you go with me now," Luke held out his hand, "or take a chance on how I will react. Will I let you live so you can screw your son another day or will I throw your hypocritical, suddenly God-loving butt in the fire with your friend?" Luke suddenly grinned. "That was some show he put on, wasn't it? I don't think I've had one quite that animated in a thousand years or so." The grin faded. "Think hard, Juan, before you answer. Will you join me in my Kingdom?"

Juan saw the stricken faces of Loam and Zeus in his mind, reminded himself of the years he'd spent as a homosexual, defying the Scriptures, speaking proudly for it and...inadvertently leading others down the same path of sin. My God, how many men *had* he converted with his writings? Was he redeemable? Better yet, was he strong enough to risk either consequence—living to eventually rape his precious Loam or dying unwillingly in the fire?

Juan stared at the red mass of lava rising and bubbling in the hole. He'd seen something like this once when he and Zeus had visited the volcanoes on the Fiji Islands before Loam had entered their lives. Then the guide had warned them away; said the temperatures reached greater than 450 degrees Fahrenheit. Zeus had wanted to tempt the guide; see how hot 450 degree really was. Juan had hung back. He'd felt the heat as it radiated from the angry ground. Now he was staring at its twin up close and personal.

Oh, how he wished his life had been different. How he wished he'd stood strong, stayed truer to his Catholic upbringings, ignored the gnawing need to act on his deeper, darker nature. But as the memories he'd created with Zeus and Bodie danced on his lens, he truly couldn't say he felt regret. Couldn't say he was honestly remorseful deep down in his heart where he knew it counted. Yes, homosexuality was a sin, but wasn't laying with a woman and living a lie just because it was biblically correct a sin also?

How could he claim God knowing he wasn't truly ready to turn his back on his life as he knew it? Turn his back on those who loved him in favor of Scriptures that didn't account for the world we now lived in? The hate, the vicious, barely restrained, palpable hate exhibited daily between the opposite sexes. What was holy about that? Wasn't ignoring promises and responsibilities he'd made just as bad? A conundrum any way you looked at it.

Juan knew what he had to do. His heart felt leaden as he straightened his back, stood as tall as any macho man would and said, "I'll follow you."

"No—" Deva shouted. Luke silenced her with a wave of his hand.

"One of you finally sees the light. I was beginning to wonder if the lot of you were mentally challenged or something." Luke's smile stretched from ear to ear. "It's not what I'd hoped, but it will have to do. It will definitely have to do. Ready?" He offered his arm.

Juan turned slowly, surveyed the room, the place of his last walk on earth. The suspended men, the cheap furniture, the dusty glasses, the stilled fire, all of these things he seared into his brain. Voices screeched in his head to revoke his statement, ask for forgiveness, repent immediately, but he pushed them away. There was no other way without harming those he loved the most. Damned with either option.

With tears streaming down his face, Juan took the proffered arm. Luke placed his hand over Juan's and they rose into the air…before slowly drifting into the fire-belching hole.

Fear clutched at Juan's heart. "Wait a minute! I thought I wouldn't be burned if I agreed to go with you!" he screamed as the flames inched closer.

Luke patted his arm. "Rest easy. This is the way to Hell. What? You thought we'd float away into the air?" He chuckled. "That's Heaven. We're in the opposite direction. Like I said, rest easy. No hair on your head will be burned."

Do you trust the Devil? Juan didn't. As he drifted lower, he began struggling, tried to remove Luke's hand from his arm, grasp the ledge before he sank below it.

Luke held tight; pulled at Juan's arm as his scrabbling fingers dug furrows in the pub's floor. "What is this? You've changed your mind again?"

"Yes!" For all his bravado, Hell wasn't what Juan truly wanted. He knew this now. Juan also knew there was still time. Struggling to hold onto the ledge, he threw Luke from him as he shoved his hand into his pocket, hands closing around the familiar rosary. With everything in his being, Juan twisted his head and shouted, " I stand for—" The word was forever lost as Luke roared in rage; drove his clawed hands into Juan's chest, pulled his beating heart through the decimated rib cage. Blood geysered, spraying Deva, Luke and Juan with its force. Deva whimpered, body convulsed at the sight.

Juan gasped as his breathing abruptly stopped; saw Luke's actions in slow motion before an excruciating pain slammed into his chest.

He couldn't move, couldn't think as he watched his heart pumping in Luke's hand. Saw Luke capture a large heart vein in his lips and suck until the organ paled, compressed in on itself. Could only stare incomprehensibly as Luke drew him close, bloody lips touching his in a kiss. Then everything…ceased.

Deva whimpered as she watched Luke's kiss evolve into more. His lips seemed to elongate, jaw unhinge like a snake, covering the majority of the lower part of Juan's face. Juan shriveled before her eyes as Luke's cheeks flattened inward. She heard his ragged breath over moist slurping sounds. Deva knew like she knew her own name what she was witnessing: Luke was literally sucking the soul from Juan.

Luke finally broke the contact. He pried Juan's rictic fingers from the ledge and threw him and his heart towards the fire. Watched in amusement as Juan's body somersaulted before slashing into the lava below.

Luke looked at Deva, who'd scuttled as far backwards as she could. He slowly licked his bloodied fingers, forked tongue meticulously cleaning every drop from his skin. When he'd finished cleansing his digits, he winked before he said, "Don't worry. I still got his soul," as maniacal laugher shook the building. With one last piercing gaze at Deva, who'd shrunk even further into her twisted body, he evaporated into the air, the hole in the floor vanishing in his wake.

Chapter 39

The drunk completed his fall to the floor where his glass shattered loudly upon impact. The jukebox began playing. The other man at the bar finished his laugh. The bartender placed his gun upon the counter. Jarrel stood up from the floor, scowl still in place.

"What is that smell?" Jarrel asked no one in particular. He placed a hand over his nose. Then he noticed Deva. She was huddled on the floor by the wall, her wig melted, her head twisted, her eyes scared. Blood ran from her nose, over her lips and dripped from her chin.

"Miss Deva?" Jarrel ran towards her, shoving tables and chairs out of his way. As he stared at her mangled body, he couldn't stop himself as he asked, "What the hell?" He was confused as all get out. One minute she was talking to that Ed guy and the next, her wig is jacked up, her body is twisted all weird and blood is all over her face and clothes. That was crazy!

"How'd I get down here?" the blond drunk asked his friend.

"Fell, I guess," the friend answered absently while watching the scene in front of him.

Was she electrocuted or something? Jarrel was truly stumped…then he got angry. "What the hell is going on here?" he yelled before he ran to the men at the bar. He grabbed the shirtfronts of both men and snatched them forward. "What the hell did you do?" Spittle flew from his mouth.

"Nothing man! We didn't do nothing to her! Let us go!" The blond one said.

"Not until you country hicks tell me what's going on!" Jarrel screamed in their faces.

Suddenly, the shotgun boomed. Plaster rained from the ceiling. "Won't be none of that in here! Take that shit out to the parking lot!" the bartender's voice boomed.

Jarrel released the men reluctantly. He knew they knew something. Deva couldn't be normal one second and the next, looking like she'd been dancing with the devil. He stared from drunk to drunk to the obviously high bartender, fighting the urge to punch the shit out of one or all of the men.

"Jarrel, help me. Let's go." Deva shuffled, body waddling as she walked toward Jarrel. An obscenity was uttered as Jarrel trotted forward and lifted her into his arms. He winched as her body settled abnormally into his chest, bones poking him where none should, blood smearing his shirtfront.

As they passed the men at the bar, the drunken one said, "What the hell happened to her?"

Jarrel was wondering the same thing himself.

The bartender tried to wrap his mind around what he was seeing. The gorgeous women from earlier couldn't be this freak show attraction he was looking at now. "Man, did that just happen here?" Jarrel stopped. The bartender continued before he could say a word.

"Look man, we don't have insurance for anything like that. Besides, I didn't see anything that could of happened to cause...*this.*" He waved his hand at Deva. "You men see anything?" he asked the two patrons.

"Nope," the men replied.

Deva knew she must look like the horror she'd just lived. It was evident in their eyes. She avoided glancing in the mirror as she rasped, "This has nothing to do with you. Let's go, Jarrel."

"Oh, okay then," the bartender said to Jarrel's retreating back. "Come back again!" he added for good measure as the door was closing behind him. Turning back to the men at the bar, he told them, "Time to go, boys. This night has been a long one...for some reason."

Chapter

40

Jarrel was beside himself as he tried to position Deva on the backseat. *What the hell happened here? How can she be normal one minute and the next this…this mess?* No matter which way Jarrel turned her awkward body, the seat belt didn't fit normally. He finally pulled out his penknife and cut the seat belts, tying them around her twisted appendages to hold her in place. He couldn't bear the thought of hitting a bump or swerving and Deva catapulting to the floor.

#

Deva never said a word as Jarrel shifted, pulled and finally tied her into place. Her mind was on what she'd just endured. No horror she'd even imagined competed with what she'd witnessed. The Devil. Hellfire. Watching life being sucked from a human. It was like one of the scary movies she avoided viewing. Only worse. She closed her eyes and prayed.

Dear God, I am so sorry. So, so sorry about everything—the fornication, the misleading of others, every sin known and unknown. Please, let me get through this. Please don't leave me in this state. I'm your child. Your prodigal daughter.

Please forgive me. I stood and proclaimed that I wanted you. Just give me the vision, the blueprint, show me the path. I promise never again to forsake what I know to be right for quick riches. If anyone can reverse what Luke said, it's you. I am grateful for this life you have given me. Give me a chance to show you. And…please God, please don't let me stay this horrid cripple I am now! Please! Amen.

She hoped God heard her.

#

Jarrel closed the door after tying Deva in then suddenly stopped. He stared at the car parked behind him then walked further back and looked in the parking lot. Five cars left—four of which had been there when they arrived and a new one behind his—and only three people inside. Deva said the others had left. He looked up and down the dark road, no houselights winking in the night. But that didn't make sense. If they'd left, *how* did they leave?

Goosebumps broke out on his skin, the hairs on his neck stood at attention. Something was definitely wrong, not just with Deva's condition, but the entire thing. That guy Ed, where was he? Where had he vanished to leaving Deva a holy mess? If he and she were as close as she claimed, why hadn't he stuck around?

Jarrel finally shook his head and walked back to the car. The first thing on his list was getting Deva to a hospital. Maybe they could tell him what was going on.

#

Deva watched the forest pass beyond the window. The trees seemed to bow, reach down as the car traveled the foggy road. She noticed a deer standing on a hill, head lifted in their direction, eyes glowing in the night. *An omen?* Then a sign was headlighted: INTERSTATE 92 SOUTH, 1 MILE. She sighed. Civilization again.

As they rounded a curve, a car sitting half-way onto the road suddenly came into view. Jarrel swerved hard away from the stalled car. Instinct made Deva reach out, try to brace herself and surprisingly…she did. Her twisted limbs had somehow *straightened*, allowed her the ability to push against the door; stopped her from hitting her head.

"Jarrel! I can move!" she yelped in surprise. *Thank you God!* She'd heard of prayers being answered, but…this quickly?

#

Jarrel heard her but his attention was drawn back to the road as a little girl darted away from her mother and into the road beside the car. The small brown face was spotlighted in the headlights as the mother grabbed the little girl's sweater; pulled her close. A man changing a tire yelled something he couldn't hear but from the look on his face, he was admonishing the child as Jarrel would have done with his own children.

Jarrel crawled along until they'd passed the danger point before he turned to Deva. He was stunned at what he saw: She was flexing her arms like she was doing aerobics. One minute, she couldn't move much more than one muscle, now entire body groups were working again. He didn't know what to make of it, couldn't wrap his mind around the entire concept, hell, he didn't want to figure it out. One thing for sure, once he got Deva situated, he was looking for another J-O-B.

#

"Jarrel, did you hear me? I can move!" Deva shouted again. She flexed her twisted ankle, was encouraged to continue as it…shifted. Righted. *ThankyouGodthankyouGodthankyouGod!* She tentatively began to rotate her head, slowly, carefully. She stopped as she felt the pop in her neck…*Don't let me down, God, not now! Not when I need you the most!* …then began again, determined to see if it was her imagination. It wasn't. In seconds, her neck worked as normally as it always had.

Deva clapped her hands together like an exuberant child. "Yes! Yes! We can skip the hospital. Take me to the hotel!"

#

Jarrel could only watch mutely as Deva "unshrunk", elongated back to her original form. But it was only when she peeled the burned skin from her face that he almost lost it. It was like watching the Bride of Frankenstein turn into the Beauty Queen. His dinner swirled up his throat as she lifted the blackened skin and crumbled it in her hands.

Lord, I just want to be home. Whatever mess went on tonight, I want no parts of. Just help me to get to the hotel. I'll take it from there.

#

Deva untied the seatbelts from her torso, giggling in happiness at her returning normalcy. She flexed and arched. Turned and twisted to ensure herself it wasn't her imagination. She prayed fervently as the car zoomed along, ignoring Jarrel in her excitement.

#

Jarrel had the accelerator pressed to the floor. He'd watched, stomaching roiling, as Deva contorted this way and that in the back seat. He wondered, truly wondered, if the *real* Deva was gone and some demon-possessed being had replaced her. His skin crawled as he too prayed to see the lights of the city; something that would tell him he was reaching the end of this nightmare.

Finally, the hotel came into view. Jarrel didn't realize how fast he was driving until he saw pedestrians scrambling from the roundabout in front. He slammed on the brakes, leaving at least ten feet of skid marks on the concrete in his wake. He dropped his head onto the steering wheel as the car stopped inches from a pillar. *Thank you God.* His part of this nightmare was over.

#

Deva jumped from the car as it halted. She took no notice of the gasps of surprise as she skipped into the hotel lobby. She waved off the 'Ma'am do you need a doctor?' call from the desk attendant as she entered the elevator, repeatedly stabbing her floor level with eager fingers.

Deva ignored the look of horror on the elderly matron's face as she bounded from the elevator and trotted to her room. She beat on the door and was elated when Lena opened it. Deva said nothing as she ran to her bed and fell on her knees.

She'd learned.

Epilogue

Archives Retrieval. 6/15/05. www.SouthBeachChronicles.com.

BODY IDENTIFIED

The decomposed body found on West South Beach has been identified as Broderick Rush, university professor. School officials indicate Dr. Rush had taken an extended leave of absence for an undisclosed illness. Cause of death is under investigation.

****

13 January 2006. CONSOLIDATED NEWSWIRE.

PASSING OF A LEGEND

Whitehall Fordham, the Silver Tongued Fox of radio has died at 90. This legendary radio owner, often chastised for his controversial DJ's, ruled the airways during this country's most segregationist years. His skirmish with the NAACP after broadcasting the hanging of a black man brought him national attention.

Mr. Fordham was removed from life support last night after a very short illness. The cause of death is suspected to be a brain aneurysm. An autopsy is pending.

In lieu of flowers, the family requests that donations be made to the WHITEHALL FORDHAM CHILDREN'S FUND created shortly before his death.

Mississippi Newslink **January 15, 2006**

Man Found Dead in Apartment Complex

Edward Burris, a resident at the Oak Hill apartments was found dead this morning. Police were called because of the odor emanating from his apartment. Mr. Burris' body was found in the bathtub. It was readily apparent that he had been dead for a few days. The coroner has ruled the death a suicide.

****

IP Wire. January 17, 2006. Top Radio Host Missing

Tab McGrifth, the flamboyant radio host of *Living Life as your Right* has been reported as missing. Mr. McGrifth has not been seen since January 12th, his last broadcast date.

Tab McGrifth is the best known prodigy of the late Whitehall Fordham, the segregationist radio owner of numerous stations throughout the south.

There was no sign of forced entry at his home but his 2004 Mercedes has not been located. Foul play is suspected. The police are following any and all leads.

OUT NEWS TODAY. **7/5/2006 Evening Edition**

WHERE IS JUAN RODRIGUEZ?

By Sam Caesarea

Juan Rodriguez, best-selling sister author and one of the most vocal proponents of same sex marriage has not surfaced after five months. Despite the strident pleas of his live-in lover, police seemed to have made *NO* progress in discovering his whereabouts.

Is this normal operating procedure? To just be lax about a person missing? I think not! This is a travesty! We should all be outraged that for some reason—most likely the fact he is a homosexual—this obvious crime has not been properly investigated!

Despite the heterosexual view that homosexuals often run off for no good reason, this is not true. *Especially* in this case.

Fact one: Juan Rodriguez was involved in a "committed relationship" and according to his partner, marriage had been discussed.

Fact two: Juan Rodriguez spent thousands of dollars with a surrogate in order to become a father. His son is now six years old. What father would run off and leave his child?

Fact three: No credit card in his name has been used and none of the money he amassed from sales of his best-selling novels has been touched.

Does this sound like a man gone underground? Like someone having a mid-lover crisis? You and I both know it is not.

People, it is up to us to place continued pressure on our officials to correct these oversights! I hope that you will join me by signing my petition located at my site, www.samceasarea.com. It is my wish that soon I will wake up without the same burning question on my mind: Where *is* Juan Rodriguez?

World Press Entertainment News. November 30, 2006.

She's Back!

Hold onto your seats, folks! Deva, the pop goddess who dropped out of the entertainment world earlier this year claiming she had a spiritual revelation, has resurfaced!

Deva's sold out engagement at the Majorca Dome shows this diva has returned better than ever. No, there was no boob exposure…but it was close! Deva strutted out in a sumptuous flesh-toned body suit that left mouths watering and bodies writhing with the need to get closer. Her voice was CD perfect.

Deva's highly anticipated new release, *Back from Hell*, sold almost a million copies in the first week.

Watch out, folks, ain't no stopping this diva!

International News. December 25, 2006.

DEVA INDICTED!

Deva, hip hop princess, has been charged with involuntary manslaughter in the death of Jimmy Tomahawk. Mr. Tomahawk, best known for exposing Deva's boob at the 2004 Superball halftime show, was found hanging in her hotel room December 1st following her comeback concert at the Majorca Dome.

Rumors of the two's involvement when Mr. Tomahawk was a minor have bounced around for some time. Both parties previously denied this information. However, it has been confirmed that the two superstars were vehemently arguing at an after concert party. Though speculations are plentiful, the cause of their argument is not known. What is known is that Jimmy Tomahawk's body was found after his mother, Maria Tomahawk, lead paparazzi to Deva's hotel room in search of her son.

Maria Tomahawk said she'd hoped to expose the 'blatant lie that is Deva's life' to the world. "She is just a child molester. A bold faced child molester who corrupted my sweet Jimmy. I hope she fries in Hell."

Deva and her lawyer have declined an interview.

Acknowledgements

First, I must humbly thank God for giving me my talents and allowing me to use them. I also am thankful to the entire Tillman family as well as the Morris-Vaughn extended family for their wholehearted support.

Many thanks to the book clubs who have sponsored me, chosen my books for their clubs and just opened their minds to my writings. I have to give a special "Thank You" to the Jackson Mississippi Reader's Club for their continued, unwavering support for my works. A big thank you also goes out to the bookstores who allowed me to sign at their venues. I'm happy you took a chance on me!

I would also like to thank Carol King Brooks, my former publicist, for her insight, guidance and encouragement as I navigated the murky waters of self-publishing. Missing you, chick.

Let me give a shout out to all the authors who have befriended, lent an ear, given encouragement and just propped me up when I was down. Much love to JY, Lesley Hal, The Too Sexy For You Writers crew, Black Expressions and Writersrx writing groups and the members of Sydney Planet! Special thanks to my tour partners, Maseyree and Tina Brook McKinney. *Mucho* love to the ladies of the SwacPage.com.

I have to give much gratitude to the Alcorn State University Writing Lab for editorial pointers and critiques. Thank you Dr. Cindy!

Last, but not least, I must thank Mr. Byron Hamberlin, my cover model, for his patience during the photo shoot and his positive attitude about the entire endeavor. I owe you one.

And as always, keep on writing because I plan to keep on reading!

Sydney Molare, www.sydneymolare.com

March 2006

A Fishbowl International Readers Guide To

Devil's Orchestra

Sydney Molare'

A Conversation with Sydney Molare'

1. How was Devil's Orchestra *born?*

Honestly, *Devil's Orchestra* is my wake up call to the world. We now live in a society where anything goes and no one seems to be willing to "just say No" to the over-the-top acts which are continuously flaunted in front of us. In fact, people seem to embrace them. The wilder the stunt, the better we tend to ingest the story. I just wanted to have my say on the subject. I used orchestra in the title because the characters in the book are like "first chair" musicians in an orchestra—you can always count on them to deliver. If the numbers had to be whittled down, these would be the ones the conductor would like to have left. Tab, Deva and Juan were first chair in the Devil's orchestra. Their actions had increased his Kingdom by millions thus, the reason Luke had to personally return to escort them into the Kingdom. They were his superstars.

2. Were your character based on people you know?

No people I know *per se*. However, *Devil's Orchestra's* characters were based on people we see and read about daily. I just compiled their actions and antics into one person.

3. Some will classify this book as Christian fiction. Is it?

More like quasi-Christian fiction. The undertone is spiritual in nature but the presentation of the message—language, situations— is quite spicy.

4. Did you know how the book would end when you began writing it?

No indeed. I actually outlined the earlier chapters but once Luke stepped into the picture, the entire flavor of the book changed. I never planned to make him as compelling as he became nor did I expect his actions in the end.

5. *Speaking of Luke, why did you make him so "human?"*

I think people are always under the impression the Devil will only appear with cloven hooves, horns and a tail. If we remember scripture, Lucifer was quite beautiful. I wanted to give him this humanness so that readers would connect and understand the Devil *can* look like you and me.

6. *How long did it take you to complete this novel?*

Much longer than anticipated. Why? Writing about the Devil made me quite nervous. I encountered a mental "roadblock" I was reluctant to cross. So it actually took me an extra year to find the courage to finish it.

7. *What message do you hope people take away from reading* Devil's Orchestra?

That every action has a reaction and repercussion to someone, including the person generating the initial action. So while we may not think further than the initial action, the aftereffects can be quite damaging to someone else down the road. For example, Tab's initial foray into broadcasting caused an innocent man to be killed. Deva's antics have millions of girls following her lead just like many pop divas today. We can all attest to the half-dressed girls roaming the streets believing their body is the *only* thing they have worth offering to someone. Juan wrote a book that, while allowing people to "see" the truth about themselves, caused families to be torn a part. Were the end results their initial goals? No. But the results still occurred.

QUESTIONS FOR DISCUSSION

1. Success can be defined many different ways. While I used money, fame and prestige, what other ways can one define a person as being "successful?"

2. Can you list the seven deadly sins?

3. Which character's ending surprised you the most? The least?

4. In your opinion, why does a person pray to God in the midst of crises yet seem to "forget" about him when the crisis is over? Why don't the original lessons (i.e. Ten Commandments) "stick?"

5. What state first allowed same sex marriage?

6. What is worst? A gay person marrying the opposite sex knowing they are still attracted to the same sex or living life as an openly gay person? Why?

7. What is your opinion on same sex partners raising children? Do you believe it affects the children? Leads them to a life of homosexuality?

8. Can you identify any of the persons used to make each character's composite?

www.ingramcontent.com/pod-product-compliance
Lightning Source LLC
LaVergne TN
LVHW091045080826
845145LV00002B/628

* 9 7 8 0 9 7 6 5 6 1 9 1 0 *